Falcon Hollow

A Historical Perspective

D. Patrick Dillon

FALCON HOLLOW ARCHIVES

Volume I

Falcon Hollow: A Historical Perspective

© 2026 D. Patrick Dillon

Published by Falcon Hollow Publishing

ISBN: 979-8-9946362-2-0 (e-book)

ISBN: 979-8-9946362-3-7 (paperback)

First edition

Dedication

For my parents, who taught me how to keep going even when the ending wasn't clear.

PROLOGUE

A Configuration

This record did not begin as an idea.
It began as a pause.

After the years that rearranged Falcon Hollow without ever fully announcing what they were rearranging, motion no longer felt like understanding. Events accumulated faster than explanation could keep pace. The familiar responses—naming, summarizing, moving on— began to feel less like clarity and more like habit. Each attempt to keep up produced a thinner account than the one before it.
So the only useful response was to slow down deliberately.

There were no deadlines attached to that decision. No expectation of resolution. The work did not arrive with instruction so much as permission. It did not announce itself as necessary. It simply refused to be rushed.
Look again.
Not at what happened.
At what remained.

Falcon Hollow already lives inside its own record. It does not require reconstruction. The streets remember. The lake reflects. The station holds. The walls carry. These are not metaphors so much as functions the town performs without ceremony. Memory here is not preserved for display. It is embedded.

Nothing in Falcon Hollow disappears cleanly enough to require commemoration. What fades does so by compression, not erasure. What endures does not announce itself. It continues because it remains useful, legible, or structurally necessary. Loss is absorbed without punctuation. Continuity does not need to be declared.

This has always been true of the town, though it is easier to recognize after disruption than before it. During years of relative calm, continuity passes for inertia. Only when pressure is applied does its shape become visible.

What had not been done—at least not deliberately—was to place these elements beside one another and observe the pattern they form. That is the work that follows.

The choice to assemble rather than summarize is not aesthetic. It is methodological. Chronology suggests causation where there may only be accumulation. Narrative implies resolution where none is guaranteed. Falcon Hollow does not behave according to those assumptions. It does not unfold cleanly. It layers.

What appears here is not organized for drama. It is organized for function. The town as stage. The roles that persist. The spaces that absorb pressure. The routines that continue without requiring explanation. The forms of attention that survive because they are useful, not because they are celebrated.

These are not subjects.

They are positions.

Falcon Hollow is composed of positions that predate their current occupants and will outlast them. A counter must be kept. A road must be patrolled. A record must be maintained. A place must remain open long enough for someone else to rely on it. The town does not require permanence from individuals. It requires only that someone is always willing to step into the spaces continuity creates—and remain there long enough for pressure to settle instead of disperse.

This distinction matters. It explains why Falcon Hollow produces few legends and many placeholders. The town is not structured to elevate personalities. It is structured to preserve alignment. When one person leaves, another assumes the posture. When a function falters, it is noticed not because it is absent, but because the pressure redistributes elsewhere.

That redistribution is how Falcon Hollow signals change.

This account is not a conclusion.

It is a configuration.

Nothing here is offered as definitive. The purpose is not explanation, but alignment—the deliberate act of placing familiar structures into adjacency so the town's logic can be seen briefly instead of simply felt. This is not an attempt to settle meaning. It is an attempt to make its contours visible.

The elements themselves do not change by being placed this way. What changes is their relationship to one another. A street remains a street. A building remains a building. A year remains a year. But proximity alters emphasis. Patterns emerge not because they are named, but because they have always been present, waiting for sufficient stillness to be noticed.

Falcon Hollow does not resolve under scrutiny. If anything, it deepens. Coherence here is not static. It moves. It accumulates. It resists final phrasing. Attempts to reduce it to explanation produce only partial truth. Attempts to leave it untouched produce only familiarity.

Between those impulses—analysis and acceptance—this work situates itself.

The choice to assemble rather than narrate is also an acknowledgment of scale. Falcon Hollow does not operate at the tempo of places built for recognition. Nothing here requires immediate comprehension. Consequence arrives slowly and remains long after attention would normally move on. What matters most in the town is rarely what travels farthest.

Durability here is not romantic. It is practical. Things last because replacing them would introduce more instability than repair. People remain because departure would create obligations elsewhere that

cannot be easily filled. The town teaches restraint not through doctrine, but through repetition.

This work does not end with an announcement, because the town does not. There is no final chapter waiting to be written, no decisive turn that resolves the pattern into a lesson. The lake will continue to reflect without commentary. The streets will continue to bend light. The station will continue to manage pressure. The walls will continue to hold what they are given.

None of these functions require recognition to persist. They only require occupancy.

This record exists because someone paused long enough to assemble what usually remains scattered. Long enough for adjacency to replace urgency. Long enough for endurance to reveal its shape without insisting on interpretation.

Nothing more was required.

PART I
THE LAND THAT PERMITTED SETTLEMENT

Before Falcon Hollow developed streets, buildings, or institutions, it was already defined by the terrain that gathered them. The basin, the ridges that surround it, and the water that collects at its lowest point shaped how movement occurred here long before anyone attempted to organize that movement into a town. The following chapters examine the conditions that made settlement possible, beginning with the land itself and the quiet authority it continues to exercise over everything built within it.

Chapter 1

Basin, Ridge, and Waterline

Falcon Hollow exists because the land allows it.
That allowance is narrow. Conditional. Specific.

From a map, the town appears gathered—streets tightening as they approach the lake, roads curving inward instead of extending outward, development settling into the basin as if guided there deliberately. What looks intentional from that distance is something else when experienced on foot. Movement slows without instruction. Sound behaves differently. Sightlines shorten. You don't arrive at Falcon Hollow so much as you are received by it.

The hollow is not dramatic. It does not announce itself through elevation or drop. A shallow bowl formed by low ridges and wooded rises holds the town without enclosing it fully. The land does not trap.
It contains.

That distinction matters, because containment allows movement while still influencing its shape.

Water occupies the lowest point. Everything else arranges itself around that fact.
Climbing the ridge clarifies what the basin conceals.

The ascent is gradual at first, then steeper than expected. Underfoot, shale loosens easily, shifting in thin sheets that fracture under pressure. Roots surface where soil thins. The forest canopy opens incrementally rather than dramatically. You do not realize how high you have climbed until the lake comes back into view from above.

From that vantage, Falcon Hollow appears smaller than it feels from within it. Streets compress into curves. The lake flattens into a dark oval set within lighter ground. Rooflines cluster more tightly than they seemed at eye level. The ridges opposite reveal themselves as boundaries rather than background.

Beyond them, the land continues—but not invitingly.

The basin sits in the fold between larger corridors. To the south and east, terrain rises toward more populated valleys. To the north, the forest thickens toward state lines that matter administratively but not topographically. The hollow is closer to borders than to centers. It belongs more to the ridges than to the highways that skirt them.

Sound does not travel upward easily. From the ridge, the town feels suspended rather than active. Movement below becomes pattern rather than detail. The lake holds light differently from that elevation, reflecting sky in muted planes rather than rippled fragments.

From above, containment becomes visible.

The hollow is not isolated. It is insulated.

And insulation is different from remoteness.

Leaving the basin requires effort in a way arriving does not.

Roads that enter Falcon Hollow descend gradually, guided by contour and drainage. Roads that leave it climb. The shift is subtle but persistent. Engines work slightly harder. Curves tighten before straightening. Tree lines draw closer before thinning.

The difference is not dramatic enough to register as difficulty. It registers as adjustment.

Travel outward feels longer than it measures. The ridges do not block passage, but they insist on ascent before release. Once beyond them, the land opens into broader valleys where movement quickens and sightlines extend farther than they do within the hollow. Sound travels differently there. Wind carries with less interruption. Development gathers along flatter corridors where roads run straighter and destinations announce themselves earlier.

From within Falcon Hollow, those corridors feel distant even when they are not.

The basin sits closer to forest than to interchange. Closer to state lines than to city centers. Closer to water and ridge than to grid and signal. None of these proximities are extreme. They are simply weighted.

The hollow does not prevent access.

It slows departure.

And slowing alters perception.

A drive that would feel brief across open valley stretches feels transitional when it begins with ascent. The ridges recalibrate expectation before the wider landscape reappears. By the time broader corridors come into view, the hollow already feels behind you—even if you have traveled only a few miles.

Insulation works this way.

It changes scale without changing distance.

The basin that holds Falcon Hollow was shaped by water long before it held roads or addresses. Runoff gathered here because it had nowhere else to go. Streams braided and slowed, depositing silt that softened the ground enough for roots to take hold. Over time, the land learned how to collect without collapsing. That lesson remains embedded in the terrain.

The lake at the western edge of town is not large by regional standards. It does not dominate the landscape. It occupies it. Fed by creeks that gather before committing to direction, the lake absorbs excess quietly, then releases it downstream at a pace that rarely draws attention. The shoreline shifts seasonally, but never urgently. Rocks move. The waterline changes its posture. The lake remains.

Fog forms most reliably near the water. It collects there in the early morning, thickest at the edges, thinning as it drifts inland. Some mornings it lifts quickly. Others it lingers just long enough to soften the first hour of movement. It does not obscure so much as it dulls. Edges blur. Distances compress. People adjust their pace without discussing it.

The effect is subtle, but cumulative. Over time, the land teaches patience without instruction.

The ridges that ring the basin serve as quiet limits. They do not loom dramatically, but they insist on scale. On clear days, they define the edges of what feels reachable. On overcast ones, they dissolve into low cloud, leaving the town suspended in something that feels both enclosed and unanchored. Perspective here is conditional.

The roads respect that lesson.

They follow the contours of the land rather than correcting them. Curves appear where straight lines would have required insistence. Intersections hesitate. Routes bend around drainage, stands of older trees, and shallow depressions where water once lingered longer than planned. Efficiency has never been measured here by time alone. It has been measured against disturbance.

As a result, movement through Falcon Hollow is adjusted rather than constrained. Cars slow without signage. Pedestrians linger without intending to. There are few long sightlines, fewer places where you can see far enough ahead to anticipate arrival. Most destinations reveal themselves late.

This is not coincidence. It is geology.

Sound behaves the same way. It does not carry far. It settles. Noise dissipates into trees, water, and uneven elevation. What remains audible tends to be close and immediate. Conversations feel local even when they are not meant to be. Silence here is not emptiness. It is absorption.

Winter reinforces these boundaries without spectacle. Cold tightens materials and narrows movement. Wood contracts. Metal stiffens. Ground hardens unevenly. Some years, snow arrives heavily enough to quiet the town completely for a day or two. Plows fall behind. Power flickers. The hollow fills with enforced stillness.

Then it lifts.

Roads narrow instead of closing. Sidewalks demand caution rather than avoidance. Travel resumes with attention rather than urgency. Falcon Hollow does not shut down for winter. It waits it out.

Summer applies pressure differently. Heat settles into the basin and lingers longer than forecasts predict. Air grows heavy near the waterline. Afternoon storms gather without hurry and release themselves with little warning. Thunder rolls against the ridges and dissipates before it can gather force. The land absorbs noise as readily as it absorbs runoff. Spring does not arrive as color first. It arrives as release.

Ice withdraws unevenly along the basin floor. Ground that appeared solid in late winter softens in sections where drainage lingers. Footing becomes uncertain along the lower paths near the lake. Shallow depressions fill again before committing to dryness. What felt firm in February requires reconsideration in March.

The ridges respond differently. Snow melts there first, exposing leaf litter and shale sooner than the basin floor. Water runs downhill in narrow, temporary channels that disappear as quickly as they form. Creeks swell not violently, but persistently, reclaiming width that winter had narrowed.

The basin breathes out.

Autumn performs the opposite motion.

Light thins before temperature drops. Visibility briefly expands as leaves fall from the canopy, opening sightlines that were concealed all summer. The hollow feels larger for a few weeks—ridges clearer, distance easier to measure. Then the ground fills with what the trees have released.

Footing grows louder.

Dry leaves gather along road edges and collect in the shallow folds of the basin. Wind moves them in slow drifts that reveal subtle elevation changes otherwise unnoticed. The lake lowers slightly, exposing stones that had been submerged. Edges sharpen again.

The basin contracts inward before winter tightens it.

Neither transition is dramatic.

Both are corrective.

They remind the town that stability here is seasonal, not fixed. That what appears solid in one month will loosen in another. That even containment shifts at its margins.

This pattern—pressure applied, pressure dispersed—repeats across seasons. It trains a particular relationship to disruption. Nothing here arrives cleanly enough to demand dramatic response. Everything arrives gradually enough to allow adjustment.

The hollow does not reward insistence. It rewards listening.

Over time, that listening produces a particular spatial literacy. Residents learn where fog thickens first, where ice lingers longest, where water pools after storms. They learn which roads clear fastest and which require patience. These details are not taught formally. They are absorbed through repetition.

The land does not explain this lesson. It repeats it.

Long before there were buildings to anchor movement, the basin shaped it. Routes formed where crossing was easiest. Paths followed water because water already knew where to go. High ground offered orientation without separation. What came later adjusted to those conditions rather than replacing them.

From within the basin, this training is easy to miss. It takes time to notice that you have stopped expecting speed. That you measure distance differently. That waiting has become ordinary rather than frustrating. These changes are not conscious. They are environmental. You learn them by staying.

There are mornings when the fog lifts just enough to reveal the lake without clarifying its edges. The surface holds the sky imperfectly, reshaping light into something flatter and quieter. On those mornings, the town feels suspended—assembled, but not asserted. The ridges remain. The roads wait. The water holds.

Nothing asks for attention.

Falcon Hollow exists where the land permits settlement—but only on its terms. Those terms have never changed. They have simply waited to be recognized.

The basin does not close.

It holds.

Chapter 2

The First Names (and the Names Before Them)

Falcon Hollow was not named first.

Long before it learned how to call itself anything at all, it was already being used. Movement preceded settlement here. That much is evident even now, if you look at the map without asking it to explain itself. The most persistent lines are not property boundaries or street grids. They are curves—paths that follow water, rise gently with the land, and pass through places that still feel like crossings rather than destinations.

Those routes did not begin with ownership. They began with knowledge.

The basin was never empty, though later records would imply it was. Water dictated approach. Ridges offered orientation without enclosure. The lake's edge provided meeting ground that did not require permanence to function. People moved through this place because it allowed movement, not because it demanded settlement.

The land was legible before it was named.

Before there were houses along the lake, before there were lots measured and subdivided, the hollow functioned as a point of passage. It was not remote enough to discourage movement, nor central enough to demand permanence. It offered what corridors offer: shelter without obligation.

Seasonal movement reinforced this character. During wetter months, higher ground along the ridges provided stable travel. In drier periods, lower crossings became reliable. The basin allowed choice, but only within the limits it set. Passage required attentiveness to contour and drainage. There were easier ways through, and there were costly ones.

A corridor is different from a frontier. A frontier invites conquest. A corridor requires negotiation. Those who moved through the hollow did so because it was useful, not because it was empty. It provided orientation between more fixed destinations. It linked rather than anchored.

That distinction matters.

When later settlement occurred, it inherited a place accustomed to transition. The hollow had already learned how to accommodate movement without demanding permanence. Early structures aligned themselves along established routes not because of sentiment, but because deviation meant unnecessary labor. The land had already demonstrated where weight could rest and where it should not.

Even now, the town retains that corridor logic. Traffic enters and exits more often than it accumulates. Roads funnel rather than fan outward. Movement feels guided rather than expansive. Falcon Hollow did not begin as a point of origin. It began as a point along the way.

That history remains embedded in how it holds people—not tightly, but conditionally.

The original names for this place are largely absent now. They were not preserved in plaques or formal record. They were spoken. When the speaking stopped, the language thinned and eventually vanished. What remained was use.

Spoken names behave differently than recorded ones. They do not depend on uniform spelling or formal recognition. They persist through repetition—passed from one voice to another, adjusted slightly each time until their edges soften. Over time, pronunciation shifts. Consonants flatten. Vowels stretch or collapse to accommodate unfamiliar tongues. Meaning erodes first. Sound lingers longer.

Creeks tend to retain older sounds more stubbornly than streets. Water resists standardization. It does not require signage to remain relevant. A ridge can be renamed without altering its posture, but a watercourse demands to be referenced in the same places it always has been. When settlers adapted earlier names, they did so unevenly. Some sounds survived intact in local speech even after maps corrected them. Others were simplified for record-keeping, shortened to fit within the margins of deeds and survey lines.

Language bent the way roads bent.

At some point, a spoken name required ink.

The act seems minor in retrospect—a clerk seated at a desk, copying sound into form—but it altered permanence. A creek long identified by rhythm rather than spelling became fixed in letters that could be filed, indexed, and referenced later without memory of how it had first been pronounced.

Spoken names adapt easily. They stretch to fit the speaker. They absorb accent. They soften consonants that do not travel well between languages. But paper demands selection. One spelling must be chosen over another. A vowel must settle. A consonant must either remain or disappear.

The decision is rarely ceremonial.

It is practical.

A surveyor submits field notes. A clerk transcribes them into a deed. A mapmaker shortens a longer word to fit within the margin of a printed plate. A syllable drops because it complicates alignment. A compound name becomes singular because repetition feels inefficient.

None of these alterations announce themselves as change.

Yet each one narrows possibility.

Over time, what was once a flexible sound becomes a fixed reference. Later generations assume that what appears on the map must have always appeared that way. The earlier variations are not contested. They are simply forgotten.

Creeks hold memory longer than roads because they are referenced more often in movement than in ownership. A person must know where water runs in order to cross it safely. A ridge may be renamed without altering its use. A crossing cannot.

But even water yields eventually to record.

A name spoken differently by successive generations can survive quietly until documentation standardizes it. Once standardized, deviation appears incorrect rather than original.

The hollow did not object to being named.

It absorbed the name the way it absorbed boundary lines.

The sound remained in local speech for a time, bending around the printed version before gradually aligning with it. What endured was not the first pronunciation, nor the last.

It was the function the name continued to serve.

Not all names were carried forward equally. Those tied to utility endured. Those tied to narrative faded more quickly. A crossing used daily retained its designation because people needed to agree on where it was. A seasonal gathering place might be remembered only as long as the generation that relied on it remained present. When reliance shifted, the name went with it.

What survives in Falcon Hollow tends to do so because it remains operational.

There is no singular preserved vocabulary for what preceded formal settlement. The hollow did not organize its earlier knowledge for posterity. It passed it along as needed. Some fragments remain embedded in altered creek names or older property descriptions. Others survive only in pronunciation habits that no longer correspond to written form.

Records attempted to stabilize these fluctuations. Clerks selected spellings. Surveyors defined edges. Maps fixed letters in place. But the land did not adjust itself to match documentation. It continued responding to sound, weight, and repetition rather than ink.

There is a difference between naming something and knowing how to move through it.

The earliest human presence here understood the basin in practical terms. Where water deepened after rain. Where footing failed in thaw.

Where elevation offered perspective without exposure. Those details did not require inscription to remain meaningful. They were corrected through consequence rather than recorded for preservation.

Later names layered over that knowledge. They did not erase it. They compressed it.

The first survey lines did not glide across the basin smoothly.

They were carried.

A measuring chain stretched between two men does not ignore contour simply because a map will later flatten it. It catches on roots. It dips into shallow depressions. It must be lifted over stone and reset where footing fails. Stakes driven into damp ground hold less securely in thaw than they do in frost. A corner marked in early spring may shift by summer.

Ink dries more quickly than soil stabilizes.

On paper, boundaries appear deliberate. Straight segments imply authority. Angles suggest decision. But the act of marking those lines required negotiation with terrain that did not share the same priorities.

A ridge that looks minor from a distance becomes significant when a line must pass over it. A drainage path that appears incidental on a dry day becomes obstruction after rain. Surveyors learned quickly that intention and contour do not always align.

Adjustments followed.

A boundary nudged to higher ground to avoid seasonal flooding. A line redrawn to respect an established path rather than interrupt it. Measurements repeated when frost heave lifted earlier markers out of place. Maps were amended not because they were incorrect in theory, but because the ground insisted on revision.

The basin did not resist being divided.

It required accuracy.

What was written first was not always what remained.

When survey lines were first drawn across the basin, they followed intention more than contour. Straight boundaries appeared on paper even where the land resisted them. Property corners were marked with stakes that did not always correspond to stable ground. Over time, these abstractions adjusted.

Boundaries that ignored drainage patterns required revision. Lines that cut too cleanly across slope encountered erosion. Access routes shifted slightly to accommodate seasonal flooding. Maps were updated. Descriptions amended. Parcels subdivided and recombined in response to terrain rather than theory.

Documentation bent.

This was not an admission of failure. It was recognition of authority.

The land did not protest in language. It corrected through persistence. Water pooled where it always had. Frost heaved in familiar depressions. Soil loosened along predictable gradients. Surveyors returned. Measurements were refined. The paper changed more often than the ground did.

Falcon Hollow did not resist mapping. It absorbed it.

But absorption is not submission. The basin continued shaping outcomes long after boundaries were inked. Deeds passed between owners. Structures changed hands. The routes connecting them remained largely intact.

Settlement followed existing cues rather than replacing them. Inheritance occurred without emphasis. Continuity persisted without proclamation.

Memory here survives through alignment, not explanation.

Names will continue to change. Businesses will rotate. Addresses will be reassigned. None of that disrupts the routes that still guide movement through the basin. People follow them without knowing why. They pause where others paused. They gather where gathering has always been easiest.

What mattered here was never what this place was called.

It was where it allowed passage—and where it did not.

Even now, movement through Falcon Hollow obeys rules older than its name. Roads bend where the land insists. The lake anchors approach. The ridges limit vision gently but firmly.

The land was still setting terms.

What survives longest is not what was written down.

It is what continued to work.

Chapter 3

Weather as a Local Authority

In Falcon Hollow, weather does not arrive as an event.

It arrives as instruction.

Forecasts matter less here than familiarity. Residents know what the basin will do before a screen confirms it. Clouds gather differently over the ridges. Storms hesitate at the hollow's edge. Cold settles unevenly, pooling where elevation allows it and lifting only when the land decides it has lingered long enough.

The hollow moderates extremes without eliminating them. Heat does not scorch so much as press. Cold does not strike so much as constrict. Wind rarely howls; it redirects. The terrain breaks momentum into manageable pieces, forcing weather to negotiate its passage the same way people do.

Weather here does not announce itself.

It repeats.

Winter

Winter enforces the clearest terms.

Cold arrives gradually enough to be anticipated. Wood tightens. Metal contracts. The ground hardens unevenly, exposing weak repairs and forgotten seams. Nothing collapses dramatically. Instead, everything becomes slightly less forgiving.

Movement narrows. Footing matters more. Sounds carry farther in cold air, but fewer of them are made. Speech shortens. Effort becomes visible.

Snow is rarely catastrophic, but some years it accumulates in volume enough to close roads briefly and quiet the town completely for a day or two. Plows fall behind. Power flickers. Travel becomes impractical.

The hollow fills with enforced stillness.

There are days in winter when snowfall begins before anyone remarks on it.

The first flakes do not demand adjustment. They drift lightly, visible only against darker surfaces—car hoods, evergreen branches, the exposed grain of porch steps. Roads remain wet rather than white. Movement continues as usual, though headlights flick on earlier than necessary.

By mid-morning, accumulation becomes measurable.

Tire tracks leave clearer impressions. Side streets grow quieter as errands are postponed without discussion. School dismissals are considered. The air thickens slightly, not with wind, but with presence. Sound softens. Even distant traffic seems closer because there is less of it.

Snow settles differently across the basin.

Higher ground along the ridges gathers accumulation first. The lowest stretches near the lake hold moisture longer before committing to coverage. Sidewalks shade unevenly, freezing faster where buildings block the sun. Steps require testing before weight is fully applied.

By early afternoon, the town recalibrates.

Plows begin their circuit, not urgently but methodically. Their routes follow known priorities—main corridors first, then secondary roads, then residential stretches. The work is repetitive and unspectacular. Snow piles along curb lines. Intersections narrow temporarily. Driveways become small negotiations between effort and patience.

Inside homes, the light changes.

Windows brighten without direct sun. Rooms reflect white from outside, softening edges and flattening contrast. Time feels slowed not because clocks move differently, but because external cues have been reduced.

By late afternoon, snowfall often tapers without ceremony.

The hollow grows quiet enough that individual movements stand out. A shovel against pavement. A door closing. A boot scraping snow from a threshold. No one hurries. There is nowhere urgent to reach.

Evening arrives earlier than usual.

Streetlamps cast halos that expand outward, catching snow still suspended in air. The lake becomes indistinguishable from shore, its surface blending into the field around it. The ridges fade into low cloud.

Nothing dramatic has occurred.

No infrastructure has failed.

No declaration has been made.

Yet the town has adjusted fully.

Travel has been reconsidered. Plans rescheduled. Movement reduced. By the time the snowfall ends, the hollow has already absorbed it into routine.

The following morning, plow lines define passage again. Roads are narrower but usable. Footprints mark successful crossings. Life resumes not because winter relented, but because its terms were acknowledged.

Snow does not conquer Falcon Hollow.

It instructs it.

Then the weight lifts.

Roads narrow instead of closing. Sidewalks demand caution rather than avoidance. Movement resumes without urgency. The town does not treat these interruptions as exceptional. They are understood as part of the contract the land occasionally enforces.

Falcon Hollow does not shut down for winter.

It waits it out.

Weather does not punish here. It trains.

Spring

Spring does not arrive cleanly. It unsettles rather than renews.

Freeze and thaw loosen what winter tightened. Pavement cracks widen. Mud persists longer in shaded stretches. Creeks swell—not violently, but insistently. Water remains high just enough to discourage assumption. The land resists clean transitions. It insists on overlap.
This is when patience is tested most often.

Schedules stretch. Repairs are delayed. Projects pause without ceremony. The town does not interpret these pauses as failure. They are understood as provisional, expected, temporary.
Spring teaches restraint by refusing to stabilize quickly.

The ground must decide it is ready before anything else can proceed. People learn not to force readiness. They learn to observe it.

Summer

Summer applies pressure differently.

Heat settles into the basin and lingers beyond sunset. Air grows heavy near the lake. Humidity flattens sound and dulls edges. Midday becomes inefficient.
Routine adjusts without announcement.

Work begins earlier. Evenings stretch longer. Activity compresses around shade and water. The lake absorbs noise and returns it softened. Even gatherings feel subdued. Nothing is prohibited. Everything is merely slowed.

Afternoon storms build slowly along the ridges, release themselves, then retreat. Thunder rolls across the hollow and disperses before it can gather force. Rain falls steadily more often than violently. Streets shine briefly, then dull. Creeks rise predictably. Water collects where it always has, then moves on when capacity allows.

The town knows which intersections hold water longest and which drain first.

Detours are made instinctively.

Fog is the most consistent authority.

It gathers overnight near the waterline and moves inward without urgency, softening outlines and muting distance. Headlights remain on longer. Conversations begin closer together. The town does not treat reduced visibility as disruption. It treats it as condition.

Fog does not demand acknowledgment.

It assumes control.

There are mornings when the fog does not lift on schedule.

It gathers overnight along the waterline as it always does, but instead of thinning with first light, it settles inward and remains. The lake disappears first, though it remains exactly where it was the evening before. Shoreline vanishes. Dock posts fade into suggestion. The opposite bank dissolves entirely.

Sound changes before visibility does.

Engines start and idle longer. Doors close more deliberately. Footsteps on gravel feel amplified because they are closer than expected. Conversations shorten not from impatience, but from proximity. You speak to the person beside you, not across distance.

Headlights remain on past mid-morning.

Roads do not close. They narrow perceptually. Curves arrive later than usual. Landmarks appear only when you are nearly upon them. The ridges that define the basin recede into blankness, removing the sense of boundary without removing the boundary itself.

The hollow feels larger and smaller at the same time.

Drivers adjust without instruction. Speed decreases not because of signage, but because certainty decreases. A familiar route requires renewed attention. A turn you have taken for years demands confirmation. The town moves, but carefully.

By late morning, the fog may begin to thin.

Not dramatically. Gradually. Rooflines reappear before trees. Trees emerge before ridges. The lake returns last, flattening light into silver rather than reflecting sky.

Nothing in the town has changed position.

But for several hours, orientation was conditional.

That conditionality instructs.

Residents do not interpret fog as disruption. They treat it as a temporary recalibration of distance. Appointments are delayed without resentment. Deliveries arrive when they can. Outdoor work pauses until edges sharpen again.

When the fog finally lifts, the hollow feels restored, though it was never truly obscured—only softened.

The ridges return. The lake reasserts itself. Sightlines extend.

But memory of the compression lingers.

The next time fog gathers, no one is surprised.

They have already been trained.

Autumn

Autumn narrows the light.

Leaves thin the canopy. Visibility increases briefly, then contracts again as the ground fills with color and sound. The season carries the illusion of clarity while introducing brittleness in advance.

Preparation begins quietly.

Wood is stacked. Gutters cleared. Small repairs made before cold exposes them. No announcements accompany this shift. It happens because it has always happened.

The cycle repeats without deviation.

Repetition as Authority

Over time, these patterns become instructional. Not in the way rules instruct, but in the way habits form.

The town learns what can be done quickly and what cannot. What must be planned for and what can be improvised. What will wait and what will not.

Authority here did not originate in offices or ordinances.

It originated in predictability.

Because seasons returned reliably, restraint became ordinary. Urgency never became the default language here. When disruption occurred—mechanical, social, institutional—it was evaluated against patterns already proven.

Reaction was tempered by memory.

Escalation was reserved for moments that truly required it.

Most did not.

The land does not demand obedience.

It demonstrates consequence.

Every fogbound morning, every narrowed road, every delayed thaw reinforces the same lesson: permanence here is conditional. Stability depends on adjustment. Movement requires listening.

By the time formal structures arrived—governance, zoning, public schedules—the posture was already embedded. The town did not need to be taught restraint. It had rehearsed it season after season.

Weather does not simply pass through Falcon Hollow.

It trains it.

And what it trains is not resilience in the dramatic sense, but alignment—the quiet, repeated decision to move when movement is possible and wait when it is not.

Authority here does not announce itself.

It returns.

PART II

STRUCTURES THAT OUTLAST PURPOSE

Once settlement took hold in Falcon Hollow, the land's influence did not disappear. It simply shifted form. Buildings rose where terrain allowed them, and over time those structures began carrying memory in the same quiet way the basin carried water and weather. Some continued serving their original function. Others adapted, paused, or endured beyond usefulness altogether. The following chapters examine how Falcon Hollow's built environment absorbed change without erasing what came before, allowing the town's history to remain visible in the structures that still shape its movement.

Chapter 4

The Mill That Wouldn't Fully Die

The mill did not begin as a landmark.

It began as a solution.

Water slowed naturally where the creek bent south of the basin, gathering enough force to be useful without demanding control. The site did not need to be discovered. It had already announced itself through repetition. Logs caught there. Ice thinned there first in spring. Sound carried differently along the bank, carrying farther downstream than upstream. The land revealed its tolerances long before anyone measured them, long before survey stakes were pressed into damp soil.

When the mill rose, it did so because the land had already agreed.

Early records describe it in practical language—output totals, ownership transfers, repair intervals, the cost of iron brackets and timber beams. There is no ceremonial account of its construction. No speech preserved about what it meant. The mill existed to convert motion into labor. That was justification enough.

Its placement was deliberate. South of the lake's curve, beyond the last residential stretch and the bend where pavement narrows into county blacktop, the ground lowers toward the creek and the forest presses closer. The building stands at that thinning point—at the edge of town, but not beyond it. Close enough to serve Falcon Hollow. Far enough that dust, noise, and runoff would not settle over Main Street.

In winter, wind from the trees reaches the structure before it reaches the road. In summer, shade lingers longer there than it does downtown. The mill sits in that subtle temperature shift where town air becomes forest air.

The lower level was constructed from red stone blocks—thick, uneven, and set with the assumption of endurance. Each stone carries slight irregularities, surfaces chipped and re-seated as needed during original construction. Above it rose hand-hewn wooden siding, later weathered into muted gray-brown, grain raised by decades of rain and sun. The roofline dipped gradually with age but never surrendered. A massive waterwheel, darkened by moisture and iron staining, still turns when spring rain swells the creek enough to wake it.

The structure was designed for strain.

Inside, the logic of its construction remains visible. Heavy timber beams span the workshop floor, cut wider than modern standards would require. Iron brackets reinforce joints where vibration once demanded tolerance. Peg holes mark earlier configurations where equipment was shifted rather than replaced.

Light behaves differently inside the mill than it does in town. Morning enters through upper windows in angled shafts, catching suspended dust and illuminating tool outlines left on walls. Afternoon light settles lower, touching the stone foundation before climbing the beams. In overcast weather, the interior dims quickly, and shadow pools in the corners where old pulleys hang motionless.

The main level is long and open, built for repetition rather than ornament. Tools once hung in ordered rows; some remain in place, their handles worn smooth by use. Pulleys creak when touched. Hooks protrude where belts once ran. The loft above narrows toward the roofline, accessed by a staircase steep enough to discourage casual traffic. Its boards retain the slight indentation of boots that climbed them daily.

Below, the stone foundation descends into a colder understructure where water seepage never fully dries in summer. Even in July, the air carries a faint chill. The smell there is mineral and timber combined—a residue of years when grain dust mixed with moisture and settled into the mortar.

The building was never decorative.

It was mechanical.

For decades, it performed exactly as intended. Grain arrived by wagon, wheels grinding gravel into the approach path. Horses stamped near the entrance while sacks were unloaded. Inside, wood strained against water-driven force. Grain left altered. Tools arrived dull and left sharpened. The sound of work—wood under tension, metal under friction, water striking paddles—folded into the town's daily rhythm until it ceased to draw attention.

Children walking the southern road learned to recognize its sound before they understood its purpose. Residents adjusted their errands around its steady operation. The mill did not define Falcon Hollow's identity so much as support it without announcement.

That adaptability became its defining trait.

When larger downstream operations introduced efficiencies the hollow had never prioritized, the mill's public function narrowed. Production slowed, then ceased. Machinery quieted. The creek did not. What followed was not abandonment in the conventional sense.

The mill did not pass cleanly from use into disuse. Its role fragmented. Seasonal crews continued to sharpen tools there. Equipment was stored and retrieved in cycles. A door hinge was replaced. A window boarded and later unboarded. A padlock appeared and disappeared. The building continued to work in parts long after it stopped working as a whole.

Ownership transferred on paper without transformation. Assessments were commissioned and deferred. Renovation proposals surfaced and stalled. A sign announcing "Future Development" stood briefly at the roadside before weather reduced it to splintered wood.

Each generation assumed the next would determine its fate.

No one did.

This indecision was not neglect. It was recognition without articulation. The mill occupied a position the town had learned to respect: present, heavy, resistant to urgency. Removing it felt disproportionate. Altering it felt unnecessary. Leaving it alone felt correct, even if no one could clearly explain why.

The creek reinforced that posture.

In heavy rain, water swelled beneath the wheel and struck stone with low authority. The building absorbed the force without complaint. In drought, the wheel slowed and stilled, and the mill framed the quiet rather than interrupting it. Winter froze the banks but rarely compromised the foundation. Spring thaw loosened ice in predictable increments, water lifting debris briefly before releasing it downstream. The structure did not improve the creek's behavior.

It adjusted to it.

There was a time when the mill announced the day before the sun fully cleared the trees.

Morning began with motion. Wagon wheels pressed new lines into the dirt approach. Horses exhaled into cold air. The wheel turned steadily once water flow was sufficient, the first rotations slow, then settling into rhythm. Inside, light caught suspended dust and turned it visible. Tools were lifted from pegs in practiced sequence. Work did not begin dramatically. It began predictably.

By mid-morning, the sound profile stabilized. Wood under tension. Grain poured into hoppers. A steady, repeating churn. The building vibrated subtly—not enough to alarm, but enough to remind those inside that motion drove everything.

At midday, activity peaked. Deliveries overlapped. Voices carried from interior to yard and back again. Grain sacks were stacked in orderly lines. The loft held reserves. The foundation remained cool even as the upper level warmed.

By late afternoon, departures thinned. Tools were returned. Surfaces swept. The wheel continued turning until water level dropped or light diminished enough to warrant stopping.

Evening left the structure quiet but not empty. Residual heat clung to beams. The smell of grain and iron lingered in corners. The creek continued moving whether the wheel turned or not.

That pattern repeated for years without requiring narration.

Now, a day at the mill unfolds differently.

Morning arrives without wagons. Light enters the same windows but finds stillness rather than motion. Dust settles without being disturbed. The wheel may turn after heavy rain, but its rotation no longer translates into labor. Sound is dominated by the creek alone.

Midday brings visitors occasionally—someone curious, someone remembering, someone measuring space with speculative intent. Footsteps echo differently in a room not arranged for work. Conversations are quieter, as though volume might disturb something preserved rather than active.

By late afternoon, shadows lengthen earlier than expected. Without the structure's internal motion to balance the sound of water, the creek feels louder. The forest feels closer. Silence is not empty. It is layered with what once occurred there.

Evening no longer signals the end of labor.

It signals continuation without purpose.

The building absorbs both versions of the day without preference.

Older residents remember when the wheel turned regularly—the creak of timber under rotation, the faint vibration felt through floorboards, the smell of wet grain and iron. For them, the mill represents discipline, output, repetition. It is remembered as infrastructure.

Middle generations remember it differently. As background. A place trucks parked temporarily. A storage site that never quite transitioned into something else. "Past the mill" meant you were nearing the edge of town. They recall it as presence without purpose, a structure that remained because removing it required effort.

Younger residents know it as boundary. A structure parents warned against after dark. A place where fog gathers more thickly than elsewhere. Where the forest begins to feel closer than the street behind you. To them, the mill feels withheld rather than abandoned—like something paused rather than ended.

Isolation at the edge of town has a different character than vacancy at its center. It does not appear neglected in the same way. It appears set apart.

That separation preserved it.

Grass grew higher along the stone base each year. The dirt path widened slightly from occasional foot traffic. Someone replaced a missing board on the dock-like landing near the wheel, not to restore it, but to keep it usable enough. Windows were repaired selectively, not uniformly.

The mill remained maintained enough to avoid collapse.

Over time, endurance replaced usefulness as the measure of its value.

Falcon Hollow does not fetishize its past. It accommodates it. When a structure stops producing, the first instinct is not removal but patience. Does its absence matter? Does its presence disrupt? In the mill's case, neither answer required immediate action.

Abandonment in Falcon Hollow rarely means erasure.

It means suspension.

The mill entered suspension gradually. It accumulated hesitation rather than debris. It remained part of the town's spatial grammar—paths bending around it, sightlines terminating at its walls, the creek's behavior interpreted through its foundation.

Some structures survive because they are protected.

The mill survived because it fit.

There is a difference between a ruin and a boundary marker.

A ruin signals collapse.

A boundary marker signals transition.

The Old Mill is the latter.

It stands where pavement begins to feel temporary and forest begins to feel permanent. It reminds Falcon Hollow that its growth has limits— that beyond a certain point, water and timber determine the terms.

The mill did not become sacred. It was not curated as heritage. It was tolerated as infrastructure long after infrastructure was required. It remained because the land had once agreed— and the town never found reason to disagree.

Chapter 5

Main Street as a Timeline

Main Street does not tell its story all at once.

It reveals it in fragments.

You cannot stand in one place and take it in whole. The street bends just enough to prevent a single vantage from resolving it. Buildings arrive in sequence rather than display. Brick gives way to siding. Storefronts narrow, widen, retreat, advance. Nothing announces when one era ends and another begins. Transitions occur quietly, negotiated over time rather than declared.

This is how Falcon Hollow keeps record.

If you want to read Main Street properly, you begin the way most people do—off Highway 68. The modern world releases you at the edge of town and then quickly reduces its volume. The first stretch of Main carries the last traces of speed and distance. It still remembers that it was built to move people through.

The landscape is open enough to suggest you are not yet inside something intimate. You see the town before you feel it. Trees begin to bracket the roadway. Signs appear without competition. Structures are spaced with restraint rather than urgency.

Then comes the first circle—the arrival point where Falcon Hollow redirects you. Traffic curves. Speed dissolves. Decision-making simplifies. The town does not welcome you with spectacle. It welcomes you by reducing momentum.

That is the first lesson Main Street offers: Falcon Hollow prefers you to move at its pace.

From here, the street narrows into its commercial corridor. Storefronts press closer to the sidewalk. Windows lower toward eye level. The geometry encourages walking even when drivers insist they are only running one quick errand. The architecture shifts from transitional to relational.

This is where Main Street begins to behave like a timeline.

Not a commemorative one. A lived one.

Older buildings reveal this most clearly. Their foundations sit deeper than modern codes would require—built to compensate for soil that softened after heavy rain or shifted with freeze and thaw. Upper floors were added later, then modified again. Windows moved. Entrances migrated. What looks decorative is often corrective.

Nothing here was built to be final.

Tile remains beneath newer flooring. Ghost lettering surfaces faintly in angled light. Doors hang slightly misaligned with façades they did not originally belong to. Plumbing resists modernization in certain basements. Ceiling heights constrain ambition. Load-bearing walls dictate what can and cannot become something else.

Main Street remembers through reuse.

Reuse is most visible from the inside.

Step through the door of a long-lived storefront and the layers become tactile. Floor tile sits atop older flooring, edges slightly uneven where transitions were not fully leveled. Shelving brackets remain embedded in plaster from previous configurations. A doorway framed for one business now opens into a storage room that once served a different purpose.

Ceiling panels conceal wiring that was added decade by decade, never all at once. Paint coats overlap subtly, revealing shifts in palette across eras. A wall that appears straight may bow slightly where foundation settled years earlier and was corrected just enough to remain functional.

Basements tell similar stories. Stone foundations run beneath multiple tenants. Old drain systems connect to newer piping in improvised junctions. Temperature varies from front to back room. Light fades toward the rear where original windows were once larger before being narrowed for efficiency.

Nothing inside feels temporary.

Even what was added later has aged into the structure.

Ambition adjusts to dimension. Owners design around columns they cannot move. They hang signage in locations determined decades earlier. They accept the building's proportions rather than imposing new ones.

Main Street does not erase its past.

It builds over it carefully.

A grocery became a hardware store, then an insurance office, then something quieter still. A bakery became a clothing boutique, then a thrift shop, then a seasonal retailer. Each transition left behind traces that never fully disappeared. The street absorbed change the way the hollow absorbs water—slowly, unevenly, without spectacle.

Longevity mattered more than reinvention.

A storefront that could be adapted was preferable to one that demanded replacement. Owners learned to work within inherited dimensions. Ambitions adjusted to beam placement and window spacing. Success was measured by continuity rather than expansion.

Failures did not announce themselves loudly. A shop closed. Lights went dark. A temporary sign appeared. Then something else moved in, often without altering the interior enough to erase the previous occupant's presence.

Main Street never emptied all at once.

It thinned.

This thinning created its peculiar rhythm. Activity clustered rather than flowed evenly. Certain blocks felt denser, more reliable. Others cycled through identities more quickly. Residents learned which doors opened early, which stayed lit late, which businesses endured regardless of ownership.

That knowledge circulated informally. It was learned by walking the street often enough to notice which windows accumulated dust and which never did.

Main Street changes character across the course of a day.

Early morning belongs to preparation. Delivery trucks idle briefly along the curb before engines cut. Café lights are already on. A back door opens to receive bread or produce. Someone sweeps a threshold not because it is dirty, but because the ritual signals readiness. The street feels wider at that hour. Sound travels farther. Footsteps echo lightly between brick façades.

By mid-morning, movement becomes purposeful. Doors open and close in measured intervals. Conversations happen just inside entryways. Light settles lower across storefront glass, revealing interior depth that evening will conceal. The rhythm is steady but unhurried. No one appears rushed, even when errands are brief.

Midday compresses activity without intensifying it. A few more cars circle for parking. People step in and out of shops without lingering long. The street absorbs them without strain. There is no surge, only a mild clustering that disperses naturally.

Late afternoon softens the corridor. Shadows lengthen across brick. The café window glows warmer. The barbershop window reflects more than it reveals. Movement slows again, this time toward departure rather than arrival. Lights switch off in staggered sequence. Doors lock in patterns residents recognize without needing to check.

After dark, Main Street does not disappear.

It rests.

Streetlamps cast even pools of light along the sidewalk. Storefront glass reflects the opposite side of the street, doubling its image faintly. The absence of foot traffic does not feel abandoned. It feels paused. The buildings hold their posture. The street retains its shape whether observed or not.

Morning will arrive again without announcement.

The pattern continues.

Named anchors stabilize that rhythm.

The Cedar Street Café holds its corner with quiet authority. Rounded glass softens the intersection. Morning light spills outward before the rest of downtown fully wakes. It marks a threshold—Main Street's public face meeting a side street that feels more conversational.

Across the way, the barbershop operates at human scale. Two chairs. A window that tells you whether it is busy without requiring entry. It survives not by novelty but by recognition.

These establishments store time differently than civic buildings do. They accumulate familiarity. Generations pass through their doors without requiring redesign. They remain correct even as decades shift around them.

As you continue south, Main Street's posture changes. Commerce yields gradually to administration. The street curves toward the civic circle—not as an interruption, but as a hinge.

Here, brick mass replaces display windows. Columns replace signage. The town's formal structures gather in proximity: City Hall, Police and Fire, the gazebo at the circle's center. The geometry slows vehicles without needing instruction.

Circles make you look around.

Because Main Street flows directly into this civic arrangement, governance becomes part of the timeline. Commerce, memory, and authority occupy the same route. The distance between storefront conversation and municipal decision is minimal. That proximity shapes expectation.

But Main Street does not end at City Hall.

It continues.

South of the civic circle, density thins again. This is still Main, but no longer downtown Main. Residential access increases. Intersections quiet. The rhythm shifts from clustered exchange to routine passage.

Eventually, the road bends toward the southern circle, distributing traffic toward the lake and the town's outer edges.

The map makes a point here without stating it outright:

Falcon Hollow is structured around controlled transitions.

Highway to town.

Town to downtown.

Downtown to civic.

Civic to residential.

Residential to edge.

Main Street stitches those transitions together.

It also functions as a buffer. Traffic slows here. Movement becomes deliberate. Outsiders pass through without lingering. Locals linger without explanation. The street filters attention the way the hollow filters weather.

Its walls sit close enough to discourage speed. Windows remain low enough to encourage recognition. Doorways require commitment rather than drift. Nothing invites spectacle. Everything invites presence.

Attempts at revitalization have come and gone. Banners were hung. Plans proposed. Renderings displayed. Yet each effort left the street largely intact—not through resistance, but through inertia shaped by experience. The cost of transformation outweighed its promise.

Main Street did not need to be saved.

It needed to be left intact.

Time here does not move forward evenly. It compresses. A façade updated in the 1990s may still carry the posture of the 1950s. A renovated interior may retain routines older than its paint. Meaning is relational rather than literal.

"Near the old pharmacy."

"Across from where the bakery used to be."

These references persist even after their origins fade. The past remains usable long after its signage disappears.

Main Street does not move Falcon Hollow forward.

It holds it in place long enough to remain coherent.

As long as the street continues to absorb change without demanding reinvention, the town's continuity remains intact. Buildings may change hands. Signs may change fonts. Interiors may shift.

The street itself does not hurry.

It remains what it has always been, a timeline written in accommodation rather than ambition.

Chapter 6

The Civic Core

Falcon Hollow did not build its civic center to impress.

It built it to endure.

Where Main Street bends into the civic circle, the town gathers its most deliberate architecture. Storefront glass yields to brick mass. Decorative signage gives way to column and symmetry. Commerce recedes. Presence advances.

City Hall anchors the circle.

Red brick, white columns supporting a triangular pediment, and a modest clock tower rising just high enough to mark the skyline without claiming it. The building carries early twentieth-century municipal confidence—an era that believed formality signaled responsibility. Its scale is controlled. Its placement is accessible. Governance here was designed to be reachable, not imposing.

The staircase is wide enough for gathering but not theatrical. The double doors are arched and framed in stone. The clock does not announce itself loudly. It keeps time without insistence.

Across the circle, the gazebo introduces softness to structure.

White-painted, octagonal, open to air on all sides, it sits at the green's center like a hinge between authority and community. Bands play there in summer. Brief remarks are delivered without amplification. Holiday lights are strung in winter. The structure is scaled for people rather than spectacle.

Between them stands the soldier statue—bronze elevated on a modest pedestal, flags placed seasonally at its base. It participates in the circle without dominating it. Remembrance is integrated, not monumentalized.

These elements form a configuration.

City Hall provides formal authority.

The gazebo provides communal space.

The statue provides historical acknowledgment.

None compete. All align.

The Police and Fire Department building extends that alignment physically and philosophically.

Two stories of red brick. Cream stone trim. Arched garage doors marked plainly: POLICE and FIRE DEPARTMENT. Vertical windows reinforce order. The building mirrors City Hall's material language without replicating its façade. It communicates readiness rather than grandeur.

Inside, the logic becomes even clearer.

The first floor houses shared functions. A common lobby receives whoever arrives—resident filing paperwork, visitor asking direction, responder returning from call. Dispatch operates adjacent, coordinating police and fire communications from a single room. Calls are received, triaged, routed without crossing thresholds or climbing hierarchy.

Nothing about the layout invites confusion.

Nothing encourages delay.

Fire apparatus occupies visible ground space, positioned for immediacy. Equipment is accessible without display. Vehicles depart and return without ceremony.

Above, the police department's main work area occupies the second floor. Reports are written. Briefings conducted. Investigations processed. The vertical separation is functional rather than symbolic. Emergency response begins at ground level where urgency is unavoidable. Law enforcement administration occurs one level removed, where pressure can be absorbed and managed.

Authority here is stacked, not scattered.

The arrangement reduces distance between decision and action. Administrative oversight sits within walking distance of operational response. City Hall's offices are steps away from dispatch. Paperwork does not travel across town. Neither does accountability.

This proximity shapes behavior.

Governance in Falcon Hollow behaves as maintenance rather than performance. Issues are managed. Calls are stabilized. Reports become records. Escalation is treated as failure of containment rather than demonstration of force.

The circle itself reinforces this philosophy.

Vehicles enter, curve, and exit in measured arcs. Speed dissolves without signage. Brick pavers guide foot traffic predictably. Lamp posts are evenly spaced. Benches appear where conversation might pause naturally. Even landscaping respects the geometry—greens trimmed but not ornamental, flowers planted but not flamboyant.

The design trains awareness.

The circle reveals its intention most clearly during public gatherings.

On summer evenings when a small band occupies the gazebo, folding chairs appear gradually rather than all at once. Families spread blankets along the grass. Children move in arcs that mirror the geometry of the circle itself, running the curve of the sidewalk without crossing into traffic because traffic has already slowed to a respectful crawl.

City Hall stands as backdrop rather than stage. Its columns frame the activity without dominating it. The Police and Fire building remains visible but unobtrusive, apparatus doors closed unless needed. The statue gathers quiet attention as flags shift in mild wind.

Sound behaves differently in the circle than on Main Street. Music travels outward and dissipates rather than amplifying. Applause feels contained, absorbed by brick and lawn rather than echoing sharply. Conversations layer without overwhelming one another.

When remarks are delivered from the gazebo—brief, measured, rarely amplified—the scale feels appropriate. The speaker does not tower above the crowd. The crowd does not swell beyond the space's capacity. The circle was built for this size of assembly. Not larger.

Seasonal ceremonies follow similar patterns. Wreaths placed at the statue in winter. Flags arranged in early summer. Announcements made without spectacle. The architecture does not need to transform for the event to feel official.

The circle accommodates without rearranging itself.

When the gathering concludes, chairs are folded. Blankets lifted. The crowd disperses in the same measured arcs by which it arrived. Within minutes, the green returns to its neutral posture.

The buildings remain unchanged.

Circles slow movement. Slower movement increases recognition. Recognition increases accountability. People see one another here in proximity to institutions. Authority remains visible by design rather than declaration.

Season alters tone without altering structure.

In summer, the circle feels open. Light reflects off brick and white trim. Children cross the green without disrupting traffic patterns. In autumn, fallen leaves collect along curb lines, deepening the brick's color. In winter, frost gathers along stone steps and holiday lights soften the gazebo's outline. In spring, early blooms interrupt the red palette gently.

The buildings do not transform. They absorb.

The civic core is equally instructive when nothing is happening.

Early morning, before office doors unlock, the circle feels almost ceremonial in its stillness. Brick holds the night's cool. The clock tower face reflects first light. A single maintenance vehicle may pass through, its engine briefly louder than usual in the absence of competing noise.

City Hall steps wait without audience. The gazebo stands empty but balanced. The Police and Fire lettering catches the rising sun without commentary.

By mid-morning on an ordinary weekday, activity is administrative rather than visible. A resident enters City Hall with paperwork in hand. A patrol vehicle pulls in and out without urgency. A delivery truck pauses briefly at the library entrance. None of these movements disrupt the geometry.

Winter reduces the circle further.

Snow outlines curb lines and walkway edges, clarifying the design rather than obscuring it. Footprints cross the green in diagonal paths that briefly ignore formal walkways before melting away. The statue gathers frost along its shoulders. The gazebo's railings collect thin ice that glints under pale light.

Even under accumulation, the structure holds.

After hours, when offices close and apparatus doors remain still, the civic core does not appear abandoned. It appears paused. Streetlamps define the perimeter evenly. Shadows fall predictably. The buildings hold their alignment without requiring occupation to justify themselves. The civic core was never meant to perform continuously.

It was meant to remain ready.

The Library and Post Office complete the civic cluster, smaller but aligned in scale and material. Where City Hall manages governance and Police and Fire manage response, the Library manages accumulation. Records, archives, reference materials—knowledge preserved without urgency.

Information circulates within a walkable radius.

A concern raised at City Hall becomes a call to dispatch. A response generates a report. A report becomes a record. The cycle completes without crossing large distances. Authority does not drift far from consequence.

Over time, this shapes expectation.

Residents understand governance as accessible. Emergency services as reliable. Records as preserved. Institutions are judged not by visibility but by steadiness.

This frustrates those accustomed to civic spectacle. Falcon Hollow does not advertise progress through dramatic renovation. Updates respect original palette. Additions align with existing geometry. The civic core reads as a single era extended over time rather than layered through competing ambitions.

Containment is its defining characteristic.

It contains ceremony.

It contains authority.

It contains memory.

It contains response.

And it does so without drawing attention to containment itself.

At dusk, the clock tower face grows more visible as sky dims. Lamp posts glow evenly. The gazebo becomes silhouette. The Police and Fire lettering catches ambient light. Shadows stretch across brick and grass alike.

Even then, nothing feels dramatic.

It feels deliberate.

Main Street records adaptation.

The mill records suspension.

The lake records return.

The civic core records decision.

Falcon Hollow formalized restraint by building it into its center. What the land taught through terrain and weather, the town encoded through brick, column, arch, and circle.

Presence without spectacle.

Authority without distance.

Order without display.

The civic core endures not because it is grand, but because it remains aligned.

PART III
POSITIONS THAT PERSIST

Falcon Hollow is sustained not only by its land and its structures, but by the roles that emerge within them. Certain positions appear repeatedly in the town's daily life—individuals who keep counters, moderate friction, observe patterns, and preserve what finally reaches record. These roles are rarely formalized and seldom celebrated, yet they persist across generations because the town continues to require the functions they provide. The following chapters examine how Falcon Hollow produces these positions and how, together, they shape the way information moves through the community.

Chapter 7

The Lake Places: Dock, Shop, Lodge

The lake does not sit at the center of Falcon Hollow by design.
It settles there by function.

Water gathered at the basin long before anyone thought to name it. Creeks converged, slowed, and held just enough to remain visible without asserting dominance. The shoreline did not announce itself as a landmark. It became one through repetition.
People returned often enough that its presence became expected.

Around it, a set of places formed—not simultaneously, not according to plan, but in response to the same logic that shaped the hollow itself.
The dock came first.

It began as a practical extension of shore—a way to step closer to water without surrendering footing. Early versions were shorter, narrower, rebuilt after heavy seasons. Boards were replaced unevenly. Nails driven in haste held longer than intended. Railings appeared, disappeared, returned again. No blueprint fixed its shape permanently.
The dock never became finished.

It lengthened because someone needed more room. It widened because families began arriving together. It stabilized because certain sections dipped too deeply after rain. The structure learned from use rather than instruction.
People learned it the same way.

They knew where boards flexed. Which planks warmed fastest in morning light. Where to stand when casting into deeper water. Children learned balance there. Teenagers learned distance. Older residents learned patience.
The dock rewarded familiarity.

Fishing followed not as sport at first, but as habit. Lines cast where water slowed. Pulled back when wind shifted. Tackle accumulated gradually—stored in trucks, in garages, eventually in the shop that rose nearby.

The lake offered enough to justify return without promising reward.

That balance shaped expectation.

The bait shop came next, positioned less for visibility than proximity. It opened early enough to meet the first arrivals and closed late enough to catch the last. Its porch served as an informal waiting room. Its counter organized transactions that were less economic than relational.

Inventory reflected use rather than aspiration. What sold was what worked. What did not moved quietly off the shelves. The shop did not chase trends; it responded to water conditions.

It became a ledger of routine.

Who arrived first.

Who lingered without buying.

Who stopped **coming.**

News passed through it the way water passed through the basin— briefly, leaving residue rather than accumulation. Conversations began at the counter and finished at the dock.

The shop did not host gatherings. It facilitated them indirectly. Anyone seeking access to the water passed through its orbit eventually.

That orbit widened when the lodge rose along a bend in the shoreline where water deepened and evening shadows settled earlier than elsewhere.

The lodge was never intended as spectacle. It was not a resort. It functioned as a hinge—between local and visitor, between routine and occasion. Built from timber heavy enough to suggest permanence but modest enough to avoid grandeur, it faced the lake without attempting to dominate it.

A wraparound porch extended the interior outward. Windows framed water deliberately, offering view without claiming ownership. A staircase descended toward the shoreline, acknowledging proximity rather than asserting control.

Inside, the lodge absorbed people temporarily, then released them.

Long tables encouraged assembly. Walls carried framed photographs—reunions, weddings, anniversaries—each event layered upon the last. Seasonal decorations appeared without excess. The building did not insist on attention. It waited.

Together, these places form a circuit rather than a center.

Morning at the dock becomes an errand at the shop becomes an evening gathering at the lodge. The sequence varies. The return does not. Movement among them rarely feels like transition. It feels like continuation.

The lake anchors each point without requiring acknowledgment.

Water alters the experience of these structures daily. In summer, light stretches across open surface and reflects back against dock boards and porch beams. In autumn, the shoreline tightens under foliage. In winter, ice forms along the margins, and the dock stands against it like a memory made visible. In spring, meltwater swells and carries sound farther than usual.

Sound ecology shifts with season.

The lake also shifts character across the course of a single day.

At dawn, the surface lies flatter than at any other hour. Mist gathers in low stretches along the shoreline, rising slowly as light strengthens. The dock feels colder then, boards holding the night's moisture longer than expected. Footsteps sound sharper in the stillness. Even small movements—tackle boxes set down, a thermos lid turned—carry farther than they would later.

By mid-morning, light sharpens. Glare forms across open water, narrowing vision toward the far bank. The dock warms unevenly, certain planks drying faster than others. The shop door swings more frequently. Conversation grows more practical than reflective.

Midday spreads the shoreline outward. Boats cross the surface in measured arcs. The lodge porch fills briefly with those retreating from direct sun. Water appears less reflective and more opaque, revealing currents beneath the surface rather than sky above it.

Late afternoon alters everything again. Light lowers and stretches horizontally, catching the edges of dock posts and porch railings. The lake reflects sky more fully than it did at noon. Voices soften instinctively as wind drops. Movement becomes less purposeful, more lingering.

Night removes horizon.

The far bank disappears into darkness. Dock boards cool quickly. Water absorbs sound rather than carrying it. The lodge windows glow faintly when occupied, their reflections doubling across the surface. When unoccupied, the shoreline recedes into silhouette.

The lake does not remain constant even within a single rotation of daylight.

It asks for adjustment repeatedly.

Morning voices carry outward and thin across the water. Afternoon boat wakes echo against shoreline. At dusk, conversation softens as wind settles. At night, the lake absorbs noise rather than reflecting it.

These changes teach restraint.

The lake rarely offers certainty. Wind alters surface patterns. Temperature shifts behavior. Fish respond to conditions no one fully controls. Those who insist on mastery leave frustrated. Those who adjust return the next morning.

Over time, this produces loyalty without drama.

People do not return because the lake guarantees success. They return because it offers familiarity that does not stagnate. Enough changes to remain interesting. Enough remains to feel stable.

The dock, shop, and lodge persist because they support this balance. Persistence at the lake does not mean stasis.

Dock boards are replaced in sections rather than all at once. New wood appears brighter for a season before weathering into similarity. Nails are driven where older fasteners failed. A railing repaired after storm damage rarely matches the original exactly. The dock's shape changes incrementally over decades without ever appearing redesigned.

The bait shop follows similar rhythms. Inventory thins in winter when fewer boats cut the surface. Shelves are rearranged to reflect seasonal patterns. A cooler replaced. A sign repainted. The porch floorboards sanded and sealed as needed rather than restored entirely.

The lodge closes more often in late fall than in summer. Porch chairs stack along the wall. Windows darken earlier in the evening. Maintenance crews patch roofing or reinforce deck supports during off-peak months. When spring returns, the structure reopens without ceremony, as though it had merely stepped aside temporarily.
These transitions rarely draw attention.

Regular visitors notice small differences—the new plank near the end of the dock, the shifted display near the counter, the refinished step leading toward the water—but the overall form remains intact.
The lake tolerates revision so long as it respects proportion.
Nothing here attempts reinvention.
Each structure adjusts just enough to remain usable.

Visitors experience the lake differently than residents do. For some, the water is novelty. For others, it is baseline. The lodge mediates that difference. It allows outsiders to participate without disrupting routine. Weddings and reunions pass through without altering daily patterns at the dock.
Lake places cannot withstand vacancy the way Main Street can.

If a storefront empties downtown, something eventually replaces it. If the dock stands empty for too long, absence feels immediate. If the shop closes unexpectedly, the shoreline quiets unnaturally. If the lodge darkens without explanation, the bend in the water feels altered.

Water amplifies presence and absence alike.

It reflects light back toward structures. It carries silhouettes across distance. It makes even small gatherings visible from the far bank. People see one another here in ways they do not downtown. They observe who arrives early. Who stays late. Who teaches. Who watches. The lake does not record events formally.

It records them atmospherically.

On certain evenings, when the air stills and sky lowers into gold, the dock, shop, and lodge align visually despite their separation. Light touches each surface in sequence. Water reflects structure back upon itself.

In those moments, the lake does not feel separate from Falcon Hollow.

It feels like its extension.

Falcon Hollow does not build monuments at the shoreline.

It builds habits.

And habits practiced long enough become infrastructure of their own.

The dock continues to extend outward.

The shop remains to observe.

The lodge endures to host without insisting.

The lake stays to gather and release.

Time does not pass here in marked increments.

It passes in return.

Chapter 8

The Keeper of the Counter

Every town has a place where information settles before it travels.
In Falcon Hollow, that place is the counter.

The counter appears in different forms—a diner register, a bait shop surface, a service desk, a narrow stretch of polished wood worn pale where hands rest. Its shape changes. Its function does not. It is where transactions slow just enough to allow exchange. Not of money alone, but of context.

Who came in earlier.

Who has not been seen.

What felt different this morning.

What will probably resolve on its own.

The counter does not demand conversation. It permits it.

That distinction is why it matters.

The person behind the counter learns quickly what is ordinary. The learning is not formal. It is acquired through repetition. Arrival times. Ordering habits. The way someone places their keys down. The difference between tired and distracted. The difference between hurried and avoiding.

Continuity produces literacy.

The keeper's authority does not come from title. It comes from duration. They know what is normal because they have witnessed enough variation to recognize deviation.

Customers speak differently at the counter than they do elsewhere. The posture encourages pause. Hands rest. Eyes wander toward windows or floor tiles. Words emerge without urgency. Stories are offered sideways, framed as anecdotes rather than disclosures.

The keeper does not press.

Listening here is passive by design.

That passivity is functional. People reveal more when they do not feel recorded. The counter provides that illusion. There are no forms, no files, no official memory. What is said is held briefly, weighed against experience, then either released or retained without comment.

The keeper remembers selectively.

Names matter less than patterns.

A regular who stops arriving at the usual hour.

A visitor who returns too often for coincidence.

A familiar face who avoids eye contact today.

These details are not labeled as concerns. Concern implies action. Observation does not.

Falcon Hollow does not reward premature interpretation. The keeper understands this without needing it stated. Information accumulates. It is allowed to gather weight. Only when repetition confirms it does anything shift.

Even then, movement is lateral before it is vertical.

Information shared at the counter rarely travels directly to authority. It circulates sideways first—a remark repeated casually, an observation passed along without emphasis. Context migrates through the town's informal network, gaining or losing weight along the way.

The keeper facilitates this without directing it.

They are trusted because they do not escalate. They are valued because they do not editorialize. Their role is to hold space long enough for the town to decide whether something requires attention.

This is not indifference.

It is containment.

Falcon Hollow relies on containment more than proclamation. The land taught this first. Weather trained patience. Structures outlasted their original purpose without protest. The counter extends the same ethic into daily exchange.

Not everything requires response.

Not everything needs explanation.

The keeper embodies that posture each day.

They know when silence is preferable. They know when humor deflects tension more effectively than advice. They know when a nod is sufficient acknowledgment. Their labor is emotional and invisible, measured not in solutions but in steadiness.

Most days, the work appears minor.

A cup refilled.

A receipt handed back.

A brief comment about roadwork near the ridge.

A remark about fog that lingered longer than expected.

But repetition turns minor acts into infrastructure.

The counter creates a controlled proximity between strangers and neighbors. It forces exchange without demanding intimacy. It prevents isolation from becoming complete while preventing community from becoming intrusive.

That balance is deliberate.

People come to the counter to be recognized lightly. They want acknowledgment without interrogation. They want the day to proceed without friction.

"Morning."

"Same as usual?"

"Yeah.""

You good?"

"Yeah."

The exchange may carry more than it reveals. It does not need to reveal it.

The keeper's steadiness allows compression.

When disruption does occur, the keeper often notices its outline before anyone else—not because of intuition, but because rhythm falters.

A seat remains empty too long.

A delivery is delayed without explanation.

A routine shifts without announcement.

The counter feels different.

Even then, the keeper waits.

Waiting is not negligence. It is discipline. Falcon Hollow prefers to see whether imbalance corrects itself before declaring imbalance a problem. The keeper participates in that preference. They allow silence to stretch long enough to determine whether it is temporary.

Only when absence becomes pattern does concern begin to travel.

Even then, it travels indirectly.

"I haven't seen him lately."

"Have you heard from her?"

"Strange, isn't it?"

The keeper does not present themselves as a witness. They do not claim insight. They offer recollection when asked. Their credibility rests on restraint.

This restraint protects trust.

Over time, different people occupy the position. The counter remains. New keepers inherit habits rather than instructions. They learn by watching—how to redirect without appearing to, how to let a conversation end before it hardens, how to forget deliberately.

Forgetting is part of the labor.

Not every comment deserves permanence. Not every observation requires preservation. The keeper filters without formal authority. They absorb what would otherwise circulate too quickly.

The town understands this without naming it.

Falcon Hollow cannot process daily life through official channels alone. City Hall manages governance. The Police and Fire building manages response. The library preserves record. The counter manages accumulation.

It receives what is too small for formal structure but too present to ignore.

There is a quiet cost to this position.

Staying is work.

It requires arriving when absence would be easier. It requires composure when someone else's frustration crosses the counter. It requires hearing variations of the same story without signaling fatigue. It requires neutrality in a town that prefers alignment over spectacle.

The keeper rarely receives recognition for this. Longevity is framed as personality rather than effort.

"She's always there."

"He's just that way."

The language suggests inevitability. It conceals labor.

But continuity is not automatic. It is maintained.

When a counter goes dark unexpectedly, the town recalibrates. Residents reroute. Conversations relocate. The absence feels disproportionate to the event.

It is not disproportionate.

The counter organizes the day more than most realize. It stabilizes morning. It anchors afternoon. It provides a place for small uncertainties to settle before they escalate.

Without it, attention disperses.

Falcon Hollow tolerates change. It does not tolerate vacancy easily. A closed door during expected hours creates more disruption than a public announcement ever could. The town senses coverage failing.

Because coverage is the point.

The keeper's primary function is not to sell, advise, or interpret. It is to remain. To provide a surface where the town can make contact with itself. To keep that surface available long enough for daily life to pass across it without friction.

This is why Falcon Hollow produces roles rather than legends.

The keeper is not a singular figure. It is a position the town generates repeatedly. Different voice, same posture. Different hands, same rhythm.

A counter must be kept.

Someone must agree to occupy it.

In early morning, before traffic gathers and before the civic circle begins its measured movement, the counter is lit first. Light pools across its surface. The air still holds the quiet of the hollow. Outside, fog may be thinning near the lake. Inside, the day waits.

Then the door opens.

Footsteps.

A nod.

A routine resumes.

The town proceeds because the counter is there.

Not because reassurance has been declared.

Because reassurance has been made visible.

The keeper is not symbolic.

The keeper is functional.

Falcon Hollow survives on functions.

And functions survive on people willing to stay—

long enough for the day to hold its shape.

Chapter 9

The Buffer

Some roles in Falcon Hollow are designed to be seen.

Others are positioned between forces.

The buffer belongs to the second category.

In material terms, a buffer absorbs shock. It reduces the transfer of force from one surface to another. It prevents impact from traveling unfiltered. It does not eliminate pressure. It redistributes it.

Falcon Hollow institutionalized that principle.

Scale alters response.

In places built for velocity, visibility becomes proof of function. Authority must be seen in order to be believed. Lights, announcements, visible deployment—these are treated as evidence that order is being maintained.

Falcon Hollow does not operate at that scale.

Here, visibility is measured differently. Too much display distorts proportion. Too little produces uncertainty. The town's size narrows the margin between reassurance and exaggeration. A response that would register as routine elsewhere can feel amplified here.

The buffer evolved accordingly. It moderates presence before voice is ever raised. It reduces force before it gathers. It prioritizes proportion over projection.

This is not philosophy.

It is calibration.

Law enforcement here was not built to dominate space. It was built to moderate it. The Police and Fire building sits within the civic circle, aligned physically with City Hall and within sight of the gazebo. Governance, response, and public assembly occupy the same measured radius. Authority does not stand apart from daily life. It is embedded in it.

That placement matters.

When law is positioned at the center rather than the perimeter, response becomes part of routine rather than interruption. Officers move through the same streets that lead to the diner and the library. Patrol routes overlap with morning errands and evening walks. Visibility becomes ambient.

In larger towns, law often announces itself through spectacle— lights, sirens, public statements, visible escalation. In Falcon Hollow, escalation is treated as misalignment.

The buffer's purpose is to prevent friction from accelerating.

Most disruptions in the hollow begin small. A disagreement at a storefront. A vehicle left too long along the shoreline after posted hours. Music carrying farther than intended on a humid night. These incidents rarely arrive fully formed. They accumulate through tone and timing rather than event.

The buffer intervenes early.

Not to punish.

To reduce temperature.

A patrol car slows before it stops. A conversation begins at conversational volume. The presence of uniform and vehicle is often sufficient to signal recalibration. Formal action may follow. Often it does not.

Containment is considered success.

This posture is visible in the way movement changes when a patrol vehicle is parked near the lake. Speed decreases, not from fear, but from awareness. Conversations shift in volume. Activity continues. The vehicle does not interrupt the day. It adjusts it.

Law in Falcon Hollow operates on proportion.

Too much visibility produces distrust.

Too little produces uncertainty.

The buffer must remain within narrow tolerances. Officers learn these tolerances through repetition. They patrol familiarity rather than anonymity. They know which vehicles belong in which driveways. They recognize which arguments recur and which represent deviation. They distinguish between habit and escalation.

That literacy narrows reaction.

In Falcon Hollow, distance between roles remains minimal. The person issuing a warning may stand in line later that day at the same counter as the person receiving it. Authority and citizenship are not separated by geography. That proximity discourages theatrical enforcement. It requires composure.

The architecture reinforces that composure. The Police and Fire building does not stand apart behind fencing or elevation. Its façade faces the circle directly. Brick matches the civic palette. Windows remain visible during daylight hours. Movement in and out of the structure is ordinary.

Even the circle moderates approach. Traffic curves rather than confronts. Speed diminishes before decision is required. There is no long corridor for acceleration, no dramatic avenue for arrival. Authority is encountered at walking pace.

The built environment narrows posture.

Law enforcement here is not deployed into the town. It remains within it. The physical arrangement reduces distance between intervention and observation. Presence becomes structural rather than theatrical.

Containment begins in placement.

Most days, the buffer's work appears procedural.

A noise complaint resolved before neighbors gather outside.

A traffic stop concluded without audience.

A call answered and cleared without the street ever closing.

Nothing lingers long enough to become narrative.

This is deliberate.

Falcon Hollow rarely reward confrontation. It prefers correction without amplification. When events draw attention beyond the basin, discomfort increases—not because scrutiny is unwelcome, but because scale has shifted. Amplification alters proportion.

The buffer exists to prevent that shift whenever possible.

There are moments when prevention fails.

A winter accident at the southern circle may require lights and temporary closure. An argument that begins behind a closed door may spill outward. A late-night gathering along the water may demand firmer intervention than a quiet request can accomplish.

Even then, response remains calibrated.

The goal is restoration of ordinary conditions, not demonstration of force. Streets reopen quickly. Vehicles disperse. Reports are written in measured language. Documentation records sequence rather than sentiment.

Withdrawal follows resolution.

Withdrawal is as important as intervention. Authority that lingers risks becoming spectacle. Spectacle invites reaction. Reaction invites further amplification.

Falcon Hollow avoids that sequence whenever possible.

This approach produces a specific kind of stability. It is not dramatic. It does not generate visible triumph. It produces continuity.

Continuity here is valued more than display.

Yet containment has limits.

Pressure absorbed repeatedly does not disappear. It settles. A town accustomed to minimizing spectacle may also minimize scrutiny. The same instinct that keeps disruption small can allow certain tensions to remain compressed rather than examined.

The buffer does not create those tensions.

It operates within them.

Restraint carries consequence.

A system designed to reduce amplification can also delay confrontation. When disruption is consistently compressed, patterns may remain below threshold longer than they would in places accustomed to escalation. The instinct to restore equilibrium quickly can substitute for examination.

Containment stabilizes the day. It does not necessarily resolve its causes.

The buffer does not determine which tensions merit expansion. It determines which tensions can be managed without fracture. That distinction preserves scale. It also narrows exposure.

Falcon Hollow chooses proportion over declaration. Most of the time, that choice maintains coherence. It requires vigilance elsewhere—in record, in memory, in attention—to ensure that compression does not become concealment.

Restraint is effective.

It is not neutral.

This is the complexity of restraint.

Law enforcement in Falcon Hollow functions as hinge rather than hammer. It allows motion to continue without fracture. It absorbs force long enough for other mechanisms—counters, conversations, routines— to resume their work.

When visible disruption occurs, residents recalibrate quickly. A closed road signals deviation, not crisis. A cluster of vehicles signals attention, not alarm. Once the event passes, the street resumes its posture. The buffer withdraws. Life compresses back into familiar scale.

Escalation is interpreted less as confrontation and more as imbalance—evidence that something earlier went unrecognized or unresolved. The buffer's task is not to eliminate imbalance permanently. It is to prevent imbalance from redefining the town.

Reports document what occurred. They do not narrate motive. Language remains measured. Detail is sufficient but restrained.

Documentation enters the town's archive quietly, aligned with its preference for record over rhetoric.

Authority here is most effective when it is least theatrical.

A patrol car moving slowly along Main Street at dusk is not a warning. It is coverage. It signals that friction will not be allowed to expand unchecked. The vehicle's presence communicates scale: this is manageable.

The buffer succeeds when the day continues as though interruption never occurred.

Not because nothing happened.

Because what happened did not alter alignment.

Falcon Hollow's civic core encodes this posture architecturally. City Hall formalizes governance. The library preserves memory. The Police and Fire building manages response. Each occupies a defined space within the same circle. None dominate the others. Each absorbs its share of pressure.

The buffer occupies the narrow space between disruption and disorder.

It does not eliminate tension.

It prevents tension from defining the town.

In Falcon Hollow, law is not a declaration.

It is a position.

And the position persists because it remains aligned with the hollow's scale.

Chapter 10

The Witness Class

Falcon Hollow does not centralize its knowledge.

It distributes it.

There is no single place where everything is known at once. Information does not gather in one office, one institution, or one voice. It moves through the town in fragments—seen here, overheard there, remembered elsewhere.

The hollow is small enough that distance collapses quickly. A vehicle parked along Main Street is noticed by more than one set of eyes. A porch light left on during daylight hours registers without comment. A truck seen twice near the lake does not go unrecognized.

No one announces these observations.

They accumulate.

The accumulation begins in ordinary places. The diner's stools face inward, but the front windows reflect the street. Conversations occur while eyes track passing movement. The barbershop's mirrors multiply perspective; one chair offers a view of three angles at once. At the hardware store, purchases are placed on the counter slowly enough for small talk to surface. At the lake dock, arrivals are staggered, predictable, and visible against open water.

None of these locations are designed for surveillance.

Yet all of them create it.

Falcon Hollow's scale ensures that regular presence becomes a kind of mapping. The same vehicles park in roughly the same areas. The same doors open at roughly the same hours. Children who once ran between storefronts now return with their own families. Time overlaps in physical space.

Because of this overlap, knowledge does not belong to individuals. It belongs to pattern recognition. A deviation is rarely shocking; it is first dissonant. Something feels misaligned before it is understood. The witness class responds to that dissonance quietly, adjusting expectation before adjusting behavior.

The town notices long before it announces.

The diner's front counter receives one version. The barbershop mirror reflects another. A conversation outside the post office adds context. The library desk registers who lingers longer than usual at the local history shelf. By afternoon, no one holds the full picture, yet several people hold pieces of it.

This is the witness class.

Not witnesses in the legal sense.

Witnesses in the spatial sense.

They are the regulars who occupy the same stool each morning. The barber who sees the back of every head and the hesitation before someone speaks. The cashier who notices when payment is made in silence instead of routine small talk. The neighbor who retrieves mail at the same hour each day and senses disruption before it is named.

None of these roles carry title.

All of them carry memory.

Memory in Falcon Hollow overlaps.

People share sidewalks, grocery aisles, church pews, and boat docks. They see one another in multiple contexts. A person known professionally is also known socially. A family recognized at the lake is recognized again at the civic circle. Repetition builds familiarity that no single encounter could produce.

Over time, familiarity becomes reference.

"He's usually here by now."

"She doesn't miss Sundays."

"That truck isn't local."

Statements like these are not accusations. They are adjustments to expectation. The witness class maintains those expectations quietly. They do not assemble evidence. They measure variation.

The movement of information is rarely direct.

It shifts laterally.

Information in Falcon Hollow does not accelerate. It diffuses.

A remark travels not by urgency but by repetition. It may be repeated with slight alteration, corrected by someone who knows more, or dismissed by someone who knows less. In this way, fragments are tested before they harden into assumption.

This testing is rarely conscious.

It happens in passing.

At the gas pump.

Along the sidewalk.

While returning a borrowed tool.

Because most residents share multiple points of contact, exaggeration has limited lifespan. An overstatement made in one location encounters moderation in another. A detail omitted in one conversation resurfaces in the next. The witness class functions less as amplifier and more as regulator.

Knowledge that survives this circulation tends to be durable.

It has been compared.

It has been measured.

It has been allowed to settle before being believed.

A comment offered at the diner becomes a question at the bait shop. A remark at the barbershop becomes clarification at the hardware aisle. Context migrates through informal pathways, rarely traveling directly to authority unless repetition confirms its weight.

The process is not coordinated.

It is environmental.

Falcon Hollow's scale ensures that sightlines overlap. Windows face the street. Sidewalks are narrow enough for recognition. The civic circle slows vehicles long enough for faces to register. The lake's dock gathers the same people at predictable hours. The town sees itself constantly.

That visibility does not produce constant intervention. It produces orientation. Residents know roughly where others belong, when they appear, how they move. The witness class maintains this orientation by habit rather than effort.

Most of the time, the fragments dissolve.

A truck parked out of place belongs to a visiting cousin. A late arrival is explained by weather on the ridge. A closed storefront reopens the next morning. The witness class adjusts without ceremony.

Because of this, it rarely announces itself.

Only when fragments persist do they begin to align.

A vehicle seen repeatedly at unusual hours.A routine that fails to resume.A familiar absence that stretches beyond explanation.

Even then, no one declares a conclusion. Observations are phrased conditionally. Questions are framed lightly. The witness class understands that premature certainty distorts scale.

Gossip is not the same as witness.

Gossip seeks narrative.

Witness maintains reference.

In Falcon Hollow, the difference matters. Gossip amplifies. Witness stabilizes. One demands reaction. The other records without official record.

This informal archive operates in tension with formal systems. What the witness class holds rarely appears immediately in written form. Formal record requires threshold, structure, and signature. Informal record requires repetition and proximity. The two systems do not compete; they operate on different timelines.

When something finally crosses into documentation, it often arrives already layered with context. Names are not new. Locations are not unfamiliar. The town may not have articulated its knowledge formally, but it has rehearsed it privately.

This is why official recognition rarely feels entirely sudden.

Record confirms what memory has been circling.

Reports require statement and signature. Official documentation requires threshold. The witness class operates before threshold is crossed and after it has passed. It remembers tone long after transcripts flatten it. It recalls who stood where, who spoke first, who hesitated.

No single person holds this memory completely.

It is shared.

That sharing distributes responsibility. When something feels misaligned, the witness class does not move as a body. It shifts incrementally. One person asks a question. Another confirms a detail. A third corrects an assumption. Over time, clarity emerges—not because it was declared, but because it was cross-referenced.

The town's density makes this possible.

In places built for anonymity, observation dissipates. In Falcon Hollow, it lingers. Faces repeat. Vehicles recur. Patterns become visible through proximity. The witness class relies on that proximity without naming it.

This system is imperfect.

Fragments can be misinterpreted. Familiarity can create blind spots. Repetition can normalize what should not be normalized. The same compression that protects the town from overreaction can also delay recognition.

The witness class does not eliminate error.

It narrows it.

When formal intervention finally occurs—when the buffer steps in, when record is made—the groundwork has often been laid informally. Pieces have circulated. Context has been weighed. The town is rarely entirely surprised, even if it is unsettled.

Surprise in Falcon Hollow tends to be a matter of scale, not awareness.

Residents may not know details, but they often sense shift before it is articulated. The witness class contributes to that sensing. It maintains low-level vigilance without spectacle. It observes without announcement. It remembers without archive.

Knowledge here does not erupt.

It gathers.

By the time something becomes record, it has often been memory first—shared, adjusted, refined through ordinary exchange. The witness class ensures that the town rarely confronts the unfamiliar without some prior recognition.

Falcon Hollow does not centralize what it knows.

It layers it.

And in that layering, the town keeps itself oriented—without needing to declare what it sees.

Chapter 11

The Record-Makers

Falcon Hollow keeps two kinds of memory.

One circulates.

The other is written down.

The written memory resides in quiet rooms. The clerk's office is lit evenly, not dramatically. Fluorescent light does not flatter paper, but it preserves legibility. Deeds are stamped with dates that outlive the signatures beneath them. Filing cabinets hold marriage licenses, building permits, birth certificates, transfers of ownership—paper proof of boundaries and belonging. Folders are labeled in block lettering. Metal drawers resist slightly before sliding open, as if reminding the user that access is procedural, not casual.

In the Gazette office, earlier editions rest in bound volumes. Years are compressed into spines that fade unevenly near the window. Headlines that once felt immediate now read as sequence—road improvements, school board votes, seasonal festivals, occasional tragedy flattened into column inches and format.

Church bulletins are thinner, but no less deliberate. Announcements follow structure: births, marriages, memorials, service times. Names are printed only after confirmation. Prayer requests are phrased generally. Specifics remain outside the margin.

These records do not interpret.

They register.

A parcel changes hands.

A roof is approved for replacement.

A child is born.

A resident is buried.

The language is neutral. Dates are precise. Names are spelled carefully. Signatures confirm that something occurred within the town's recognized boundaries.

This is the first distinction.

Formal record requires threshold.

Threshold is not only legal. It is cultural.

Many events in Falcon Hollow resolve before documentation becomes necessary. A dispute settled privately does not generate minutes. A rumor corrected informally does not require clarification in print. A misunderstanding resolved across a kitchen table leaves no trace in the clerk's ledger.

The archive therefore reflects resolution more often than conflict.

Tension that dissipates before formal action disappears from paper. Conversations that prevent escalation are never recorded as prevention. The town's capacity to absorb strain leaves little visible imprint in official form.

This selectivity is not manipulation.

It is filtration.

Only what hardens into decision becomes durable. What softens back into routine is carried instead—retained in memory, referenced in conversation, adjusted through repetition. The record-makers do not erase these moments. They simply operate after them.

By the time something is written, it has already crossed from possibility into fact.

Paper does not capture what almost happened.

An event must meet criteria before it becomes permanent. The clerk does not record rumor. The Gazette does not archive conversation overheard at the counter. The church bulletin prints announcements submitted, not speculations shared.

In Falcon Hollow, permanence is deliberate.

What is written becomes durable. What is durable shapes future reference. A property deed settles boundary disputes years later. An archived article provides sequence when memory conflicts. An obituary confirms lineage when stories diverge.

The record-makers do not decide what matters.

They decide what qualifies.

This difference governs the town's understanding of history. The Gazette reports on town meetings, seasonal festivals, school achievements, road closures, and elections. It notes the visible. It summarizes the resolved. It rarely publishes the unverified. Its archive presents Falcon Hollow as orderly, measured, continuous.

That presentation is not false.

It is curated by threshold.

Church bulletins operate similarly. Births, marriages, volunteer efforts, seasonal drives, prayer requests offered publicly. The bulletin reflects communal alignment rather than private strain. It documents participation. It affirms cohesion.

Clerk's ledgers are even narrower. They register compliance. A business license is issued. A permit is granted. A fine is recorded. These entries do not describe circumstance. They confirm that procedure was followed.

The form protects neutrality.

Formal record in Falcon Hollow does not chase narrative.

It marks completion.

This restraint produces clarity. Anyone reviewing the archive sees dates, signatures, and outcomes. They do not see hesitation, disagreement, or uncertainty unless those elements crossed formal threshold. The archive contains what stabilized.

What did not stabilize remains elsewhere.

The town carries memory that never reaches paper. Conversations that clarified context before documentation was required. Observations that corrected assumption before report was filed. Absences that resolved quietly without entry.

The witness class holds these.

The record-makers preserve something different.

Their work begins only after movement slows. A meeting concludes before minutes are written. A decision is finalized before publication. A transfer is complete before deed is filed. Record follows resolution.

This sequence matters.

Because it means the archive rarely captures tension in its active state. It records outcome, not process. Future readers will see that something changed on a certain date. They will not see the weeks during which that change was debated informally.

Falcon Hollow accepts this limitation.

The town does not expect its archive to hold every strain. It expects it to hold what endured.

There are benefits to this structure.

Records provide stability. They prevent reinvention of fact. They reduce reliance on memory alone. They anchor property, lineage, and governance in durable reference. When conflict arises, the archive offers sequence that memory may distort.

But record is selective by necessity.

It cannot capture tone. It cannot record hesitation unless hesitation becomes action. It cannot preserve private doubt unless doubt becomes public declaration.

In this way, formal memory is narrower than lived memory.

The record-makers understand this constraint.

They operate within guidelines designed to protect accuracy rather than fullness. They do not speculate in margins. They do not annotate rumor. They resist pressure to accelerate documentation before threshold is met.

Permanence requires patience.

The Gazette waits for confirmation. The clerk waits for signature. The bulletin waits for submission. What is not submitted does not appear.

This is not suppression.

It is structure.

Falcon Hollow's archive reflects what the town agreed to acknowledge formally. It does not reflect everything the town experienced. The difference between those two categories defines the boundary between record and recollection.

When events eventually demand documentation—when containment fails, when law intervenes, when decisions are finalized—the archive expands. New entries appear. Names are added. Dates are fixed.

Once written, they remain.

Future readers may not know the atmosphere of the moment, but they will know that it happened. That permanence carries weight. It shapes how the town narrates itself across generations.

The record-makers rarely speak about this influence.

Their authority lies in procedure.

A clerk verifies identity. A publisher verifies source. A minister verifies announcement. Each step ensures that the archive remains credible. Credibility, once compromised, is difficult to restore. Falcon Hollow protects its record accordingly.

The archive is not exhaustive.

It is durable.

Durability is the point.

Durability, however, flattens atmosphere.

A line in a ledger does not convey hesitation. A published summary does not preserve the temperature of a room before a vote. An obituary marks a life's span without recording the unresolved conversations that followed its passing.

The archive is precise about sequence and imprecise about feeling.

Future readers will know what occurred and when. They will not know how it felt to watch it unfold. They will not sense the weight of uncertainty that preceded resolution. They will encounter decision without duration.

This limitation does not weaken the archive.

It defines it.

Falcon Hollow relies on this division. The written record anchors fact. Lived memory supplies texture. Together, they approximate history more fully than either could alone.

The town's informal memory shifts as people move, age, and leave. Witness fragments disperse over time. Stories soften or sharpen depending on who repeats them. But the archive remains constant.

In quiet rooms, the town's official self waits on shelves.

What Falcon Hollow chooses to write down defines its public continuity. What it chooses not to write remains within living memory, subject to revision and interpretation.

Neither system replaces the other.

They operate in parallel.

The witness class detects variation. The buffer manages disruption.

The record-makers confirm what has crossed threshold into permanence.

Together, they define the town's understanding of itself.

The archive does not tell the whole story.

It tells the story that endured long enough to be written.

PART IV
RITUAL WITHOUT CEREMONY

Communities often explain themselves through speeches, monuments, or declarations of shared meaning. Falcon Hollow rarely does. Instead, the town reinforces its values through repetition—through fathers returning to the same shoreline, through holidays assembled the same way each year, and through places that remain legible enough for people to find their way back after long absence. The following chapters examine how these quiet patterns function as ritual in Falcon Hollow, sustaining continuity without requiring the town to announce what those rituals mean.

Chapter 12

Fatherhood as Local Currency

In Falcon Hollow, fatherhood is not debated.

It is assumed.

The assumption does not arrive in speeches or policy. It arrives in posture. In the way a man stands at the edge of the dock with a hand resting lightly on a child's shoulder. In the way tools are passed across workbenches without instruction repeated aloud. In the way a name continues from mailbox to mailbox without ceremony.

Fatherhood here is not spectacle.

It is continuity.

On summer mornings, the lake fills early with quiet exchanges that require no witnesses. Boats push off from the public dock in slow arcs, fathers adjusting life jackets, children adjusting expectations. Lines are cast not for urgency but for instruction. Patience is modeled without being labeled as such. Silence is offered as a shared activity rather than a lack of conversation.

A child learns how to wait.

A child learns how to hold the rod steady against the pull.

The lesson is not about mastery. It is about steadiness.

These mornings become evidence.

Not formal evidence. Social evidence. The kind that circulates without being recorded. Someone saw him at the dock. Someone knows he brings the kids out most Saturdays. Someone mentions it at the counter in the bait shop while coffee cools untouched beside the register.

Good man.

The phrase requires no elaboration. It attaches itself to routine and holds.

At the Falcon Hollow Bait & Sandwich Shop, mornings move in predictable sequence. The door opens. The bell above it registers entry without surprise. Coffee is poured before it is requested. Weather is discussed as forecast rather than complaint. Children trail behind fathers, absorbing the choreography of small transactions. Bait purchased. Ice scooped. Change counted.

The ritual does not declare itself sacred.

It repeats.

Fatherhood functions as visible currency in these spaces. It purchases trust without formal application. It grants the benefit of the doubt before doubt is articulated. It becomes shorthand for character.

He's a family man.

The phrase softens scrutiny. It stabilizes perception. It does not erase fault. It reorders it.

In Falcon Hollow, work and fatherhood often overlap. The mill once trained children by proximity. Not through lecture, but through exposure. A son standing near a workbench learned where to stand and when to step forward. A daughter holding a flashlight learned how long to wait before speaking. The lesson was not about gender. It was about rhythm.

Output follows attention.

The lesson transfers easily from waterwheel to garage, from workshop to driveway.

On fall evenings, fathers rake leaves into measured piles while children collapse them deliberately. Gloves are removed and replaced. Tools lean against siding between motions. The yard is restored not perfectly, but sufficiently.

Good enough carries weight here.

At the VFW hall on the Southside, fatherhood appears in quieter forms. Men sit at long tables under fluorescent light, discussing repairs and schedules more often than memory. Photographs line the walls— portraits from earlier decades when posture was more rigid and uniforms more prominent. In many of those frames, fathers stand with children gathered close, arms angled protectively but lightly.

Continuity is visible without being announced.

Service, like fatherhood, operates as proof.

Not proof of virtue, but proof of participation.

A man who shows up consistently—at work, at school events, at the dock—accumulates credibility. He may not speak often. He may not articulate intention. Presence alone counts.

In Falcon Hollow, absence is noticed slowly. Presence is assumed immediately.

This economy does not require transaction records. It operates through observation. Who stands beside whom at the parade. Who carries folding chairs from the gazebo after the fall festival. Who stays late to stack tables. Who leaves first.

These details accumulate into reputation.

Fatherhood strengthens that accumulation. It functions as multiplier.

What Falcon Hollow resists is the interrogation of the phrase good father. It accepts it as alignment with expectation. A man who coaches youth sports, who repairs a neighbor's fence without invoice, who attends school recitals without complaint—these gestures convert into social stability.

No one announces the exchange rate.

The lake reinforces it.

Fathers return to the same shoreline year after year. Children grow taller against the same dock posts. Photographs capture incremental change while preserving backdrop. A child stands where a parent once stood. A knot is tied the way it was taught.

Continuity becomes visible.

That visibility matters.

In a town where movement is guided by repetition rather than declaration, visible fatherhood reassures. It suggests the future will resemble the past closely enough to remain legible.

Blind spots form here not from malice, but from compression.

When a man is known first as father, the town arranges other information around that identity. Frustration becomes stress. Silence becomes discipline. Withdrawal becomes privacy.

The adjustment is rarely conscious.

It is protective.

Because fatherhood stabilizes so much, questioning it feels destabilizing.

Falcon Hollow does not articulate this openly. No meeting is ever called to confirm it. But the posture is visible. When a man has been seen at the dock for years, when he has been photographed beside a child at the gazebo, when he has been counted on to carry folding tables after the fall festival, that accumulation begins to function as insulation.

To examine it too closely risks unsettling more than one household.

It risks unsettling the exchange system itself — the quiet shorthand that allows trust to move quickly between neighbors. If fatherhood is not reliable, then other assumptions must be reconsidered. Presence would require interpretation instead of recognition. Routine would require verification instead of familiarity.

That kind of scrutiny slows a town built on repetition.

So the scrutiny rarely arrives unless something forces it to.

It observes.

It catalogs quietly.

It assumes alignment unless disruption becomes unavoidable.

At the Falcon Lodge, generational photographs hang in corridors that narrow slightly toward the rooms. Weddings. Reunions. Fishing tournaments. In nearly every frame, fathers stand slightly behind children, hands resting lightly at shoulder height. The posture repeats across decades. The lake remains consistent behind them.

The background does not change enough to draw attention. The faces do.

Continuity is reinforced by similarity.

Falcon Hollow does not turn these men into legends. It places them within a pattern instead. The role carries more weight than the biography attached to it. Names change. Occupants age. Circumstances vary. The posture remains. A father standing slightly behind a child in a photograph communicates continuity without requiring explanation.

Expectation attaches to that posture before character is evaluated.

They are placeholders within a role that predates them and will outlast them.

That is part of the stability.

The role matters more than the occupant.

In Falcon Hollow, fatherhood operates less as individual expression and more as structural support. It holds expectation in place. It keeps the next generation oriented toward repetition rather than reinvention.

This is not presented as virtue.

It is presented as design.

The town was trained by land and weather to prefer steadiness. Fatherhood mirrors that training. Show up. Return. Repair. Wait. Repeat.

Most men comply without drama.

Most children absorb without commentary.

The phrase good man continues circulating, attached to gestures large and small. It is spoken at counters and along shorelines. It becomes part of the town's ledger without ever being written down.

No one announces when the role is performed well. It is simply recognized.

And because it is recognized, it becomes currency.

Currency moves quietly. It stabilizes exchange. It allows transactions to occur without full disclosure of terms.

Fatherhood in Falcon Hollow functions the same way.

It reassures.

It aligns.

It holds.

Whether it always reveals what it appears to reveal is a separate question.

Falcon Hollow rarely presses the question quickly.

It returns to the lake the following Saturday.

Chapter 13

Holidays That Don't Need Speeches

In Falcon Hollow, holidays do not require explanation. They require return.

The calendar turns with little argument. Decorations are unpacked from labeled bins. Extension cords are tested and retested. Folding tables are unfolded into the same patches of grass they occupied the year before. No one drafts position statements about what these gatherings represent. The town does not interpret them aloud.

It assembles them.

Winter arrives first in the ritual year. December tightens the air around Town Circle, and the tree lighting ceremony gathers people inward. Gloves are shared. Scarves are adjusted. Someone always forgets a hat and pretends not to mind. The gazebo, framed in temporary strands of white light, becomes briefly brighter than the surrounding streetlamps.

A countdown may occur. It may not. The lights come on either way.

Applause follows, not because the illumination is surprising, but because it is correct. Children tilt their heads back to take in the height of the strands. Parents stand slightly behind them, hands at shoulder height. The Falcon Hollow Historical Dedication plaque remains mounted in its usual place, partially framed by garland that will be removed in a matter of weeks.

The Winter Festival moves between indoor warmth and outdoor cold. Cider steams in paper cups. Boots leave damp outlines along entryways. Tables are set up in the civic hall, crafts arranged in predictable rows. The decorations do not change dramatically year to year. They are stored, retrieved, rehung.

No one demands novelty.

New Year's Eve shifts the focus back toward the lake. Fireworks rise into air that carries sound more sharply in January than in July. The bursts appear brighter against the long winter dark. The reflection on the water is imperfect, broken slightly by wind or current. The echo reaches the ridges and returns softened.

The display lasts long enough to justify gathering and ends before excess becomes uncomfortable. Afterwards, cars start in staggered sequence. Headlights trace the same roads back toward North Ridge, Southside, and the wooded lanes west of town.

February brings the Love Is in the Air dance, held indoors while winter still holds the edges of the basin. Red and white decorations lean toward familiarity rather than innovation. Paper hearts appear in windows. A rented speaker hums before music begins.

For some, the dance is background noise. For others, it becomes a marker. A first slow song. A hand held longer than expected. The awkward calculation of whether to stay on the floor when the music changes tempo. Years later, someone might stand at the edge of that same room with a different partner and remember the first time they stood there at all.

No one narrates these moments publicly.

They accumulate privately.

By the third week of March, winter has loosened without fully retreating. The Spring Festival sets up around Town Circle in air that cannot decide whether it is warm or cold. Tent stakes sink unevenly into ground still soft from thaw. Streamers catch on the same railings. Banners hang from the same posts.

Children move between booths with cautious optimism, jackets unzipped and zipped again as clouds shift. Someone remarks that last year was warmer. Someone else insists it was colder. The comparison matters less than the recurrence.

The gazebo stands where it always has. The plaque remains. The brick sidewalks hold the weight of folding chairs arranged in loose arcs around temporary stages.

No speeches are required to justify any of it.

Summer expands outward toward the lake. On the Fourth of July, boats gather early, claiming familiar stretches of shoreline. Flags appear along Main Street and then disappear as quickly as they were raised. Fireworks return to the water in brighter air, their reflection stretching farther across the surface than it did in January.

Children cover their ears and then uncover them, uncertain whether the sound is part of the thrill or something to be endured. Adults clap on cue. The lake absorbs the echo and releases it in pieces.

The Summer at the Lake Entertainment Series arrives in the second weekend of August with quiet predictability. A temporary stage is assembled near the shoreline. Cables are taped down in patterns that have been tested before. Lawn chairs appear in rows that widen as dusk approaches.

Boats idle just beyond the designated perimeter, their lights forming uneven constellations on the water. The first chord from the stage travels across the lake and returns softened by distance. Applause follows, slightly delayed.

Teenagers stand in loose clusters, pretending indifference. Parents position chairs at angles that allow conversation without turning their backs entirely to the music. Someone always underestimates how quickly the air cools once the sun drops below the ridgeline.

The bands rarely surprise. They are not meant to. They are familiar enough to hum along to and distant enough to allow memory to settle without interruption. The event does not demand attention. It offers it.

Labor Day weekend marks summer's narrowing without declaring it. Long tables appear near the park. Paper plates bend under food that resembles last year's offerings closely enough to feel correct.

Conversations resume mid-sentence as though months have not intervened.

Children who were small in March are slightly taller now. The difference registers only when compared to a photograph. Someone mentions school beginning again. Someone else suggests one more swim before the water cools.

Oktoberfest follows as the air shifts toward fall. Tents line Main Street in predictable rows. Beer is poured from taps that have traveled the same route from storage to sidewalk for years. Leaves thin above Town Circle, allowing more light to reach the booths as afternoon stretches toward evening.

Music carries through streets that bend rather than echo. Laughter gathers near food stands and disperses before it becomes disruptive. Old classmates recognize one another near the gazebo and begin with the same question they asked the year before.

"How long has it been?"

No one answers precisely.

Precision is unnecessary.

What these events share is not theme.

It is recurrence.

The Town rarely shifts its calendar in response to trend or demand. It resists expansion beyond what can be assembled by familiar hands. Decorations are stored rather than replaced. Schedules are adjusted but not reinvented. When a band returns for another summer performance, no one frames it as tradition. It simply feels correct.

Repetition builds comfort without requiring articulation.

Children grow into the roles they once observed. The teenager who stood at the back of the dance floor in February may help string lights in December. The child who watched fireworks from a parent's shoulders in July eventually stands at the shoreline independently, looking out over the same water.

The setting remains consistent enough for memory to attach itself to place.

Someone remembers the year wind knocked over a tent at Oktoberfest and volunteers reset it without drama. Someone remembers snow gathering on the gazebo roof during the tree lighting. Someone remembers a slow song at the Love Is in the Air dance and the awkwardness of deciding whether to stay when the music changed.

These memories are not archived officially.

They are carried.

Their recurrence confirms their meaning without the help of speeches. The calendar advances, but the coordinates remain stable. Town Circle. The lake. Main Street. The civic hall.

When the tents come down and the lights are unplugged, nothing appears transformed. The gazebo remains. The shoreline settles. The streets resume their weekday posture.

But something has been reinforced quietly: the expectation that when the season turns again, the tables will unfold in the same places.

No one needs to explain why.

They simply return.

Chapter 14

Places People Return To

In Falcon Hollow, return does not begin with memory.
It begins with geography.

A person can leave the town for years and still know where their feet will land when they come back. The basin does not change its terms. Roads still bend where the land insists. The lake still holds the western edge of town in quiet possession. The ridges remain in the distance, not dramatic enough to be called mountains, but present enough to make the horizon feel decided.

Return is made easier by this stability.

Falcon Hollow does not reinvent itself quickly. It revises in small increments—new paint on old trim, a sign replaced where weather finally defeats it, a storefront repurposed without altering the sidewalk it faces. The result is not stagnation so much as legibility. The town remains readable to people who learned it once.

That readability is part of why they come back.

Some returns are brief. A holiday weekend. A funeral. A wedding. A visit that begins with a car parked along a familiar curb and ends with a long drive back out of the basin before daylight fades. Other returns are slower, less ceremonial: a decision made over months, a lease signed, a job accepted, a house inherited. In either case, the town receives people the same way it receives weather—without announcement.

It holds.

The first places people return to are rarely extraordinary.

They are the places that make routine visible.

Town Circle sits a short walk south of Main Street's shops, arranged around grass that stays green longer than it should in early spring and browns a little too quickly in late summer. The gazebo at its center is painted again and again, always white, always intended to look clean even when it is not. In December, light strands wrap its railings. In March, banners hang from its posts. In October, fallen leaves collect at the base steps and are kicked aside without complaint.

The gazebo does not belong to any single season.It belongs to repetition.

Nearby, the historical dedication plaque remains mounted where it was placed—steady, understated, and easy to miss if you are moving too quickly. Children climb the curb without reading it. Couples take photographs near it without knowing what it says. Tourists pause briefly, then continue toward the café or the shops. The plaque does not demand attention.

It remains.

Return to this space does not feel like visiting a landmark. It feels like stepping back into the town's center of gravity. People orient themselves instinctively here. A car parked near the circle means you are close to everything that matters in the civic sense: City Hall, the police building, the library, the post office. The institutions stand in brick and trim the way they always have—formal enough to suggest permanence, modest enough to avoid spectacle.

The town does not advertise its order.It performs it.

From Town Circle, Main Street is visible as a line of familiar fronts. The same patched brick. The same windows that reflect afternoon light at shallow angles. The same sense that the street reached its most recent version decades ago and found no reason to move beyond it. Shops change ownership. Displays rotate. Signs are updated.

But the street itself remains a timeline you can walk.

Some returns are measured in footsteps.

A person who has been gone a long time may still cross Main Street without looking for traffic first, trusting the pace of the town to remain slow enough to accommodate assumption. They may still know which side of the street catches sun in late afternoon, which windows glow first at dusk, which door sticks slightly in humid weather.

These are not dramatic memories.

They are functional ones.

Cedar Street Café sits where it always has—at the corner where Cedar meets Main, its windows serving as a lit boundary between public sidewalk and private habit. It is called Cedar Street Café on the sign. It is called Lou Whitman's Diner in conversation, as though ownership were more enduring than branding.

Inside, return is made visible through small permissions.

A familiar nod from behind the counter. Coffee poured before an order is spoken. A seat recognized as belonging to someone even after months of absence. In larger cities, this kind of recognition would be staged or transactional. In Falcon Hollow, it is simply practiced. The café does not exist to impress visitors.

It exists to hold the town's daily rhythm in place.

People returning from elsewhere often stop there first, not to announce themselves, but to re-enter the town at its most ordinary frequency. A cup of coffee. A pastry wrapped in paper. A conversation that begins with weather and ends with someone asking about a name they almost remember.

The café does not preserve the past.

It preserves continuity.

The lake is a different form of return.

It is visible from certain roads without being fully revealed. It flashes between trees and then disappears again. Approaching it requires the same patience it always has. The basin guides you there without delivering you quickly. When the shoreline finally comes into view, the effect is familiar: the water flattening light, the surface reflecting sky with imperfect fidelity.

For many residents, the lake is the first real coordinate of belonging.

They may have moved away. They may have changed jobs, accents, politics, habits. But they still remember where the public dock sits and how the boards sound underfoot. They still remember the angle of the fishing pier against the waterline. They still remember how fog gathers there in early morning and how quickly sound changes when you step closer to the shore.

Return to the lake is not always sentimental.

Sometimes it is simply proof that the town's edges remain intact.

The shoreline holds gatherings without needing to be called an event. In summer, lawn chairs appear in loose arcs. In fall, fewer people come, but those who do are quieter. In winter, the lake becomes more boundary than gathering place—still present, still visible, but less usable. Even then, people drive past it slowly, as though confirming it remains.

They do not stop.

They look.

The places people return to are rarely the places that made them leave.

Return is not an argument with the past. It is not a promise about the future. It is a brief alignment between the person and a landscape that remains legible enough to accept them without negotiation.

That legibility is built from repetition.

The gazebo lights go up each December and come down again without ceremony. The Spring Festival returns in March and leaves behind flattened grass where tents stood. Fireworks rise above the lake and fade into smoke that drifts over water. Oktoberfest tents line Main Street and then disappear, leaving only the usual storefronts and sidewalks.

What remains afterward are the fixed points.

Town Circle.

Main Street.

The café window.

The shoreline.

These places do not hold meaning because the town declares them meaningful. They hold meaning because they absorb people's lives repeatedly, year after year, without requiring explanation.

Falcon Hollow does not reinvent itself for those who return.

It offers them the same coordinates.

A person changes.

A season changes.

The town holds.

And because it holds, return becomes possible—not as a dramatic homecoming, but as something quieter and more durable.

A car turns off the highway and descends into the basin.

The road bends.

The lake appears.

The gazebo waits.

Nothing announces itself.

The place is simply still there.

PART V
SILENCE AS INFRASTRUCTURE

By the time Falcon Hollow developed its streets, its roles, and its rituals, the town had also developed a quieter system for maintaining stability. Not every disruption becomes a public story. Some are absorbed through conversation, compressed into markers on the timeline, or allowed to settle without entering the formal record at all. The following chapters examine how this habit of containment functions within Falcon Hollow—how silence, compression, and patience preserve cohesion most of the time, and how those same instincts can delay recognition when a pattern begins to emerge.

Chapter 15

What Never Makes Paper

A town produces more information than it records.

Falcon Hollow is no exception. For every event that appears in print—every council decision, every public notice, every obituary or announcement—there are dozens of smaller exchanges that never reach paper. They exist briefly in conversation, pass through the town's informal networks, and settle into a kind of shared understanding that rarely requires confirmation.

The record reflects what can be stated cleanly.

The town lives with what cannot.

This distinction is not accidental. It developed slowly, the same way Falcon Hollow's roads developed: through repetition rather than design. Over time, residents learned which things belonged in the public record and which things functioned better outside it.

Newspaper pages illustrate this boundary clearly.

The *Falcon Lake Gazette*—now simply the *Gazette* to those who have read it long enough—has always presented the town in orderly sequence. Births, graduations, council minutes, business openings, seasonal festivals. When disruption occurs, it is reported with restraint. Details are verified. Language is moderated. Conclusions remain provisional.

Paper prefers clarity.

Life rarely provides it.

The gap between those two conditions is where silence begins.

Silence, in Falcon Hollow, is not the absence of speech. People talk constantly. They talk at the diner, on the sidewalk, in hardware store aisles, across pickup beds in grocery parking lots. Conversations accumulate like weather—layered, overlapping, moving through the town in slow fronts.

But talk and record are not the same thing.

What appears in conversation may never appear in print. What appears in print may represent only the narrow portion of an event that can be verified without dispute. Between those two spaces lies a category of knowledge that everyone recognizes and almost no one documents.

The town understands this instinctively.

Some matters are simply easier to manage when they remain spoken rather than written.

Writing stabilizes information. Once printed, a statement acquires permanence. It can be archived, referenced, argued over years later by people who were never present when the events occurred. Spoken knowledge behaves differently. It adapts. It adjusts to context. It fades or strengthens depending on whether people continue repeating it.

Silence lives between those two forms.

A rumor illustrates the boundary.

In conversation, a rumor functions as possibility. It circulates lightly. People repeat it with qualifiers—*I heard, someone said, they're saying*. These phrases allow the speaker to participate in the exchange without claiming authority over it. Responsibility remains diffuse.

On paper, those qualifiers disappear.

A printed statement demands certainty: names, times, sources willing to stand behind the words attributed to them. Without those anchors, the story remains unwritten. The rumor may continue traveling through the town, but it does so without leaving an official trace.

This system is not imposed from above. It grows from habit.

Editors learn quickly that the town's tolerance for ambiguity differs depending on medium. A statement that passes easily through conversation can fracture a community if it appears in print. Once words enter the record, they invite scrutiny. They create positions people must defend.

Spoken knowledge rarely demands that level of commitment.

It allows residents to acknowledge uncertainty without forcing resolution.

The town relies on this flexibility more often than it admits.

Certain subjects move through Falcon Hollow almost entirely outside the record. They circulate through the witness class—the regulars at the café, the barbershop chairs, the people who sit long enough to observe patterns others might miss.

These observers rarely claim authority. Their knowledge accumulates through presence rather than investigation. They notice when a business changes hands quietly. They notice when someone stops appearing at the same hour each morning. They notice which vehicles pass through town repeatedly and which ones do not belong.

Observation is not accusation.

It is accumulation.

Over time, these small observations form a kind of unofficial archive. Residents draw on it when interpreting new events. They remember who was present before. They remember what happened last time a similar situation unfolded. None of this memory requires documentation to remain useful.

It simply requires repetition.

This repetition produces an unusual form of stability.

Because so much local knowledge remains informal, Falcon Hollow rarely confronts disruption all at once. Instead, tension disperses gradually through conversation. A concern surfaces at the café. It appears again later at the bait shop. Someone mentions it in passing during a council meeting without placing it formally on the agenda.

By the time an issue reaches the record, most residents have already encountered it in fragments.

The printed version does not introduce the problem.

It confirms that the problem exists.

This confirmation matters.

Once something enters the record, the town must respond to it in ways conversation never required. Officials must acknowledge it. Timelines must be established. Statements must be measured against prior statements.

Paper compresses ambiguity.

Silence resists compression.

For this reason, Falcon Hollow uses silence as a form of infrastructure. It stabilizes the town by delaying the moment when ambiguity must become fact.

Delay allows adjustment.

If a misunderstanding resolves itself through private conversation, no public statement becomes necessary. If a disagreement fades before it reaches the council chamber, the record remains undisturbed. Silence absorbs small disruptions before they accumulate into formal conflict.

Most of the time, this system works.

Problems diminish. Tempers cool. People move on.

But silence performs another function as well.

It protects.

Protection can be generous or self-serving depending on circumstance. A resident struggling privately with financial difficulty may benefit from the town's reluctance to expose personal hardship. Neighbors offer help quietly. Arrangements are made without public commentary. The individual retains dignity.

Silence allows that generosity.

The same mechanism can conceal less generous realities.

A pattern that repeats quietly may remain unchallenged longer than it should. If the town treats each instance as an isolated conversation rather than part of a larger structure, recognition arrives slowly. By the time the pattern becomes visible, it may already be deeply embedded.

This is the cost of containment.

The town values cohesion. It prefers adjustment over confrontation. Silence gives Falcon Hollow time to decide whether a disruption represents genuine threat or temporary imbalance.

But time can obscure as easily as it clarifies.

The *Gazette* sits directly on this boundary.

Journalists occupy an unusual position in towns like Falcon Hollow. They hear the same conversations everyone else hears. They recognize the same patterns circulating through the witness class. Yet they operate within a system that demands documentation before publication.

The result is a professional tension.

A reporter may know far more about an event than the paper can responsibly print. Facts must be confirmed. Sources must be willing to appear on record. Statements must withstand scrutiny beyond the town's informal networks.

Knowing something and printing it are different acts.

In Falcon Hollow, that difference becomes especially visible.

There are stories that everyone seems to understand but no one has written. There are events that altered the town's internal alignment yet produced only modest headlines. Sometimes a journalist senses the outline of a larger pattern but lacks the evidence required to present it.

The story remains unwritten.

Not because it is unknown.

Because it is incomplete.

This incompleteness shapes the town's memory.

Future readers examining archived issues of the *Gazette* may conclude that Falcon Hollow experienced long periods of calm. The paper records routine with impressive consistency: council meetings held, parades conducted, businesses opened and closed.

What the archive does not reveal is the quieter process that occurred alongside it.

Concerns were raised. Doubts circulated. Observations accumulated.

They simply never reached the page.

The town understood them anyway.

Silence, then, is not empty space within Falcon Hollow's history. It is an active component of how that history forms. It determines which events become permanent reference points and which remain part of the town's internal memory.

Without silence, every rumor would demand investigation.

Without silence, every uncertainty would require declaration.

Falcon Hollow has learned that most situations do not benefit from that level of exposure.

The town prefers to observe first.

To see whether a disturbance settles on its own.

Most do.

A few do not.

When one of those disturbances finally crosses the boundary between conversation and record, the transition feels abrupt. Residents experience the moment as sudden even if the pattern has been visible privately for months or years.

That abruptness is not the beginning of the story.

It is the moment when silence can no longer contain it.

By the time the record acknowledges a problem, Falcon Hollow already knows it exists.

The question is no longer whether the town has noticed.

The question is what it will choose to say.

Chapter 16

The Compression Reflex

Falcon Hollow rarely tells a story from beginning to end.

Instead, it reduces events to markers.

A long explanation becomes a short reference. A complicated situation becomes a point along a timeline everyone recognizes without needing to revisit the details. Over time, the town learns to navigate its past not through narrative, but through coordinates.

Before the bridge was replaced.

After the winter the lake froze solid.

That was back when the mill still ran.

These phrases circulate easily because they compress memory into something portable. No one needs to reconstruct the full history of the bridge repair or the winter freeze. The marker alone carries enough meaning to orient the conversation.

Compression functions as a kind of shorthand.

It allows Falcon Hollow to acknowledge disruption without dwelling on it.

Most communities develop similar habits eventually. But in Falcon Hollow, the process is unusually refined. Events are rarely debated publicly long enough to produce a settled narrative. Instead, the town gradually converts them into temporal boundaries—lines separating one period of normal life from another.

On one side of the marker lies the version of the town people remember.

On the other lies the version that followed.

The transition itself remains largely undescribed.

This pattern becomes visible when residents recall older incidents.

Ask two people about a flood that damaged Main Street decades ago, and their recollections will not begin with the storm. They will begin with the reference point the storm produced.

That was before the pharmacy moved.

It happened the year the high school gym flooded.

The explanation rarely extends further unless someone presses for detail. Most listeners do not. The marker has already done the work required of it. It establishes sequence. It establishes scale. It establishes that something changed.

Compression does not erase the past.

It rearranges it.

A long chain of events becomes a single hinge around which memory can turn. Once that hinge is established, everything else aligns relative to it. People remember where they lived at the time. Which job they held. Who had not yet moved away.

But the disruption itself becomes smaller.

Contained.

This containment has advantages.

Narratives require agreement. People argue about what happened, why it happened, and who bears responsibility. Markers require only recognition. A town can disagree about interpretation while still agreeing that a particular year, flood, fire, or scandal altered the landscape.

Compression bypasses the argument.

It preserves continuity without demanding resolution.

In Falcon Hollow, this method developed gradually through necessity. The town does not possess the institutional machinery required to process large conflicts in a sustained public forum. There are council meetings, of course, and newspaper coverage when events warrant it. But the scale of the town encourages a different form of response.

Problems are absorbed rather than dissected.

A disruption appears. Conversations spread. Silence does its work. Eventually the event stabilizes into a point on the timeline.

After that, the town moves forward.

Evidence of this reflex appears throughout Falcon Hollow's everyday speech.

People rarely say, remember when the diner closed for six months because of the kitchen fire. They say, that was before Lou reopened the diner.

The emphasis shifts from the problem to the restoration that followed.

Similarly, no one explains the complicated negotiations that led to the replacement of the old county bridge. The town simply references the moment the new structure opened.

That was back when we still had the old bridge.

The phrase contains the entire story without requiring anyone to tell it again.

Compression favors forward motion.

It allows Falcon Hollow to maintain continuity even when the underlying events were messy, contentious, or unresolved. By reducing disruption to a coordinate, the town limits the space available for lingering disagreement.

Once an event becomes a marker, it stops expanding.

This reflex operates most clearly when the town encounters something uncomfortable.

Small scandals, for instance, rarely develop into extended public debates. They move quickly through the informal networks described earlier—the cafés, the sidewalks, the barbershop chairs. People discuss them briefly, assess their significance, and then allow them to settle.

Weeks later, the event may already be compressed.

That was before the council reshuffle.

It happened around the time the hardware store changed hands.

The original circumstances blur. What remains is the boundary they created.

The town remembers the shift.

It does not revisit the argument.

In many cases, this approach works remarkably well. Life continues. Businesses reopen. Families remain neighbors even after difficult moments. The town avoids the cycles of accusation and counter-accusation that can fracture communities larger than itself.

Compression preserves cohesion.

But it also alters perception.

Because disruption is converted into markers rather than narratives, residents may underestimate the complexity of events that shaped their environment. The boundary remains clear. The causes that produced it become hazier with time.

Memory grows efficient.

Efficiency, however, is not the same as accuracy.

A marker tells you *when* something happened.

It rarely explains *why*.

This difference becomes significant when patterns begin to form.

If one event becomes a marker, the town absorbs it easily. If several events occur across many years, each producing its own boundary, the markers may begin to resemble a sequence.

At that point, the compression reflex reveals both its strength and its limitation.

Residents recognize the coordinates.

What they may not immediately recognize is the structure connecting them.

Falcon Hollow is particularly skilled at isolating disruptions from one another. A fire in one decade becomes a boundary unrelated to the bridge repair ten years later. A council resignation remains separate from a business closure. Each event receives its own place on the timeline without requiring the town to interpret them as part of a broader pattern. Individually, the markers feel manageable.

Collectively, they may represent something else.

Yet the town's instinct remains the same: compress first, interpret later. Sometimes interpretation never arrives.

The *Gazette* reflects this tendency as clearly as everyday speech. Archived editions record events faithfully in the moment they occur. But when readers return years later, the coverage appears episodic rather than continuous.

One issue reports a council vote. Months later another reports a resignation. A year after that, an editorial references a shift in policy. The connections between those moments exist, but they are rarely spelled out explicitly.

Readers must supply them.

This is not negligence. It is the natural outcome of reporting events as they occur within a town that prefers containment over expansion. Journalists observe the same compression reflex everyone else does.

A reporter may sense that several incidents belong to a larger pattern, but proving that pattern requires time, evidence, and sources willing to appear on record. Until those elements align, each event remains a separate entry in the archive.

The town moves on.

Years later, residents navigating Falcon Hollow's history rely on the same coordinates they always have.

Before the bridge.

After the winter flood.

That was around the time the mill closed.

Each phrase marks a hinge where the town briefly changed direction.

What the markers do not reveal is how often the town has turned.

Compression creates clarity.

It also creates distance.

By the time a disruption has been reduced to a coordinate, the urgency that once surrounded it has usually faded. The people involved may have moved away or retired. The emotions attached to the event soften with time.

The marker remains, but its edges dull.

Most communities accept this trade-off willingly. Perfect memory would make everyday life impossible. People need ways to store difficult events without reliving them constantly.

Falcon Hollow has refined that storage method into habit.

It identifies the hinge, marks the timeline, and continues forward.

The question the town rarely asks is what happens when the hinges begin to align.

If several coordinates appear close together—if the boundaries separating one period from another accumulate faster than usual—the compression reflex may begin to fail. The town can isolate one disruption easily. Two, perhaps three.

Beyond that, the pattern becomes harder to ignore.

At that point, the markers stop functioning as containers.

They begin to resemble evidence.

Falcon Hollow has not reached that moment often.

When it does, the town's instinct remains the same as it has always been.

First compress.

Then wait.

And only later—sometimes much later—consider what the coordinates might mean when viewed together.

Chapter 17

The Cost of Containment

Containment is not neutral.

Every system designed to absorb disruption carries a cost. The benefit of stability rarely appears without some accompanying form of loss. In Falcon Hollow, that loss is difficult to measure precisely because the system that produces it is the same system that prevents it from being discussed openly.

Silence protects the town.

It also limits what the town is willing to examine.

Most residents recognize the advantages first. Containment preserves relationships that might otherwise fracture. It allows neighbors to remain neighbors after disagreement. It prevents private hardship from becoming public spectacle. The town's preference for quiet adjustment keeps daily life manageable in a place where distance between people is minimal.

In communities larger than Falcon Hollow, individuals can withdraw from one another when conflict emerges. Here, withdrawal is rarely permanent. People continue to encounter one another at the café, in the grocery aisle, at school events, on the same short stretch of Main Street.

Containment allows those encounters to remain possible.

It softens the edges of conflict until coexistence becomes practical again.

This restraint is often mistaken for passivity by those observing from outside. But the residents who practice it understand that containment requires effort. Someone must decide not to escalate. Someone must choose not to repeat a rumor that would harden into accusation if spoken loudly enough.

Silence, in this sense, is deliberate.

It functions as a form of maintenance.

Over time, the town develops a shared instinct for when to apply it. Certain situations call for patience rather than exposure. A family struggling privately may benefit from the town's refusal to turn hardship into public conversation. A business owner facing temporary financial strain might recover more easily if the problem remains limited to those directly involved.

In these cases, containment operates as generosity.

The town absorbs the disruption quietly and allows dignity to remain intact.

But containment does not distinguish between problems that deserve privacy and problems that require attention. The same mechanisms that protect vulnerable residents can also shield behavior that would benefit from scrutiny.

The system operates according to habit rather than judgment.

Once silence becomes the default response, it applies itself broadly.

The cost emerges gradually.

Patterns that might appear alarming if viewed all at once remain manageable when encountered individually. A small irregularity passes unnoticed. A second incident is interpreted as coincidence. A third becomes a topic of quiet conversation rather than public concern.

By the time these events begin to resemble a pattern, the town may already be accustomed to their presence.

Familiarity reduces urgency.

This does not mean residents fail to recognize wrongdoing. Falcon Hollow possesses a strong sense of moral expectation. People notice when behavior violates the town's informal standards. They speak about it privately. They discuss it in careful language that avoids transforming suspicion into accusation.

The line between awareness and action remains narrow.

Many residents hesitate to cross it.

Part of this hesitation comes from uncertainty. Acting too quickly can damage reputations that may not deserve the damage. Once an accusation enters the public record, it cannot easily be withdrawn. Even if the claim proves incorrect, the consequences linger.

Containment avoids that risk.

The town waits.

Waiting sometimes resolves the situation. Misunderstandings clarify themselves. Rumors dissolve. People adjust their behavior once they realize it has drawn attention. Silence gives those corrections room to occur without permanent damage.

But waiting also creates opportunity.

If a pattern depends on secrecy or hesitation, containment provides both. Individuals willing to exploit that hesitation may continue operating within the boundaries the town has established for itself.

Not because the town approves.

Because the town prefers certainty before action.

This preference grows from the same impulse that shapes Falcon Hollow's newspaper coverage, its council meetings, and its everyday conversations: the belief that restraint preserves cohesion.

In most circumstances, that belief proves correct.

The town remains stable. Relationships endure. Residents avoid the cycles of public accusation that can fracture communities far larger than this one.

Yet stability can obscure smaller forms of harm.

When silence protects the community as a whole, individuals experiencing that harm may find fewer avenues through which to speak. Their concerns circulate quietly through the same informal networks that manage other disruptions. Friends listen. Neighbors sympathize.

But sympathy does not always produce intervention.

The problem remains contained.

Falcon Hollow does not consider this outcome ideal.

It considers it complicated.

Every resident who benefits from the town's protective silence also participates in sustaining it. The same instinct that shields a struggling neighbor can discourage someone else from insisting that a troubling pattern deserves attention.

Containment spreads responsibility widely.

No single person creates it.

No single person can dismantle it.

This diffusion of responsibility reinforces the town's preference for incremental response. If a situation grows serious enough, someone will eventually act. A report will be filed. A statement will be made. The matter will cross the boundary between conversation and record.

Until that moment arrives, silence continues performing its stabilizing function.

Most residents believe this arrangement remains acceptable as long as the number of unresolved situations stays small. A town can tolerate occasional ambiguity. Life continues normally when most events resolve themselves without requiring intervention.

The difficulty emerges when ambiguity begins to accumulate.

If several incidents occur within a relatively short span of time—each one absorbed quietly, each one reduced to a coordinate on the timeline—the town may discover that containment has delayed recognition of a larger structure.

At that point, the cost becomes visible.

What once appeared as isolated irregularities begins to resemble something more deliberate. The silence that preserved stability now appears to have concealed information that might have clarified the situation earlier.

Residents look back and recognize moments when questions were asked but not pursued.

They remember conversations that ended without conclusion.

They realize that the town possessed fragments of knowledge long before the full pattern emerged.

In retrospect, the most unsettling realization is not that the town lacked information.

It is that pieces of the story had already surfaced in ordinary places — remarks made in passing, small observations shared across café tables, details that seemed too minor or too strange to pursue further at the time.

None of these fragments appeared meaningful on their own. Only later, when the sequence of events was finally understood, did it become clear that the town had encountered the edges of the truth more than once without recognizing what it was seeing.

Containment does not create wrongdoing.

But it can postpone the moment when wrongdoing becomes impossible to ignore.

This realization rarely arrives dramatically. Falcon Hollow does not experience sudden revelations that transform its understanding overnight. Instead, recognition accumulates slowly as residents reconsider earlier events in light of newer ones.

The coordinates begin to align.

A conversation once dismissed as rumor acquires new weight. A detail mentioned casually months earlier begins to look significant. People revisit their memories and discover that they noticed more than they admitted at the time.

None of this happens publicly at first.

Recognition begins privately.

Residents carry it with them as they move through the same streets, pass the same storefronts, sit in the same chairs where earlier conversations once occurred. The town remains outwardly unchanged even as its internal understanding begins to shift.

This is the moment when containment reaches its limit.

Silence can absorb individual disruptions indefinitely. It struggles to contain a pattern once enough people recognize its outline. At that point, the instinct that once favored patience begins to give way to a different impulse.

Attention sharpens.

Questions that once seemed unnecessary begin to feel overdue.

Falcon Hollow does not abandon restraint easily. The town continues to weigh its responses carefully even when recognition spreads. But the posture changes. Residents begin to examine events not only as isolated coordinates but as parts of a sequence.

The timeline grows more deliberate.

When that shift occurs, the town's earlier silence takes on a different meaning. What once functioned as protection now appears as delay. The same system that preserved stability begins to feel inadequate for the moment that has arrived.

This is the cost of containment.

The town must eventually confront the possibility that the quiet adjustments sustaining everyday life also allowed certain problems to persist longer than they should have.

Falcon Hollow does not resolve that tension quickly.

It rarely resolves it completely.

Instead, the town does what it has always done when faced with something larger than its existing habits.

It pauses.

It looks again at the coordinates it has already marked.

And it begins, slowly, to consider what they reveal when placed beside one another.

The events that follow in this record are those coordinates.

PART VI
YEARS THAT BECAME COORDINATES

Historical understanding often depends on distance. Events that appear isolated when first experienced can acquire new meaning once time allows them to be viewed together. The following chapters examine several years that Falcon Hollow would later reconsider in precisely that way — moments that entered the town's history separately but gradually came to be recognized as points along the same line.

Chapter 18

2015 — A Year That Passed Quietly

In 2015, Falcon Hollow moved through the familiar rhythms that had long defined the town's sense of time. The year did not arrive with any suggestion that it would later occupy a more significant place in the community's history. To the residents experiencing it, the months unfolded in the same gradual manner that most years did: measured less by individual events than by the steady repetition of routines that organized daily life.

Winter loosened its hold slowly, as it often did in the hills surrounding the town. Snow lingered along shaded roads that ran through the wooded outskirts, while the center of Falcon Hollow resumed its usual pattern of morning deliveries and evening storefront lights. Main Street businesses opened their doors before sunrise, the café on Cedar Street welcomed early customers who preferred conversation over silence with their coffee, and the Gazette continued its weekly cycle of reporting on the matters that typically occupied a community of Falcon Hollow's size.

Those matters were rarely dramatic. School activities, municipal maintenance, and seasonal events filled most of the paper's pages. Residents read about council discussions regarding road repairs, zoning adjustments, and preparations for the summer festivals that reliably drew visitors from nearby towns. In short, the town's public record reflected a community that understood itself as stable, predictable, and largely insulated from the kinds of disruptions more commonly associated with larger places.

Communities develop expectations about the kinds of events that belong to them. In Falcon Hollow, those expectations had been shaped by decades of routine. The town's history included its share of hardships, as any community's does, but they tended to arrive in forms that residents recognized: economic setbacks, severe weather, or the occasional accident that reminded people of the risks present in rural life. Such occurrences were absorbed into the town's memory without fundamentally altering the way residents understood their environment.

It was within this context that Falcon Hollow experienced an incident that briefly unsettled the community during the spring of that year. At the time, the event was discussed with a mixture of curiosity and concern, the way unexpected occurrences often are when they first interrupt familiar routines. Conversations appeared quickly across the town's informal networks — in shops, at café tables, and in the quiet exchanges that take place between neighbors when something unusual enters local awareness.

These conversations did not immediately produce a shared interpretation. Residents speculated about what might have happened, drawing on the kinds of explanations that had historically made sense within the town's experience. Some assumed the incident reflected an unfortunate accident. Others suggested circumstances that might have been unusual but still understandable within the range of events Falcon Hollow had previously encountered. As is often the case in small communities, people relied heavily on the information available through their personal networks, where details circulated unevenly and conclusions remained tentative.

Official responses followed the established patterns of the town's institutions. Authorities addressed the matter as required, and the Gazette reported on developments with the caution typical of local journalism, particularly when information remained incomplete. The tone of those reports reflected the uncertainty that surrounded the incident during its earliest days. Without clear evidence of a larger pattern, the event appeared singular — troubling, certainly, but not necessarily transformative.

This distinction is important in understanding how Falcon Hollow processed the moment. Small communities are accustomed to disruptions that prove temporary. A single unusual event rarely compels residents to reconsider the broader assumptions through which they interpret daily life. Instead, the town's instinct is to contain the disruption within the narrowest possible explanation, allowing routine to resume as quickly as circumstances permit.

In 2015, Falcon Hollow responded according to that instinct. After an initial period of attention, the incident gradually receded from the center of public conversation. Other matters reclaimed the town's focus. The rhythms that had briefly been interrupted began to assert themselves again, and the event settled into the background of civic memory.

This process occurred quietly and without deliberate intention. No single decision caused the town to move on from the moment. Rather, the shift happened through the accumulation of ordinary days in which other concerns demanded attention. Festivals required planning, schools continued their schedules, businesses returned to the routines that sustained them. Over time, the earlier disruption lost the immediacy that had once made it a frequent topic of discussion.

By the end of the year, the incident had become something residents referred to occasionally but no longer examined closely.

It remained present in the town's memory, but it did so in a muted form — one of many events that had passed through Falcon Hollow's history without permanently altering its sense of itself.

From the perspective of those living through 2015, this outcome seemed entirely reasonable. Nothing within the available information suggested that the incident belonged to anything larger. Without additional context, the town interpreted the moment in the most limited way possible: as an isolated occurrence that, while unsettling, did not require the community to revise its understanding of the environment in which it lived.

Such interpretations are common in communities where long periods of stability shape public expectations. Residents develop a framework through which events are understood, and that framework tends to favor continuity over disruption. When something unusual occurs, the instinct is to explain it in ways that preserve the larger narrative of normalcy.

Falcon Hollow followed this pattern in 2015. The year continued along its expected course, and the town closed its calendar believing that the earlier disturbance had been an unfortunate but singular episode.

Only later would that assumption be reconsidered.

With the passage of time — and with the appearance of events that would eventually draw new attention to earlier moments — Falcon Hollow began to look back at 2015 differently. The incident that had once seemed isolated acquired a new position within the town's historical timeline. It became, in retrospect, the first point in a sequence that residents had not yet learned how to recognize.

At the time, however, no such recognition existed. The town lacked the perspective that later years would provide. Without that context,

Falcon Hollow treated the moment according to the habits that had guided it for generations.

The year passed quietly.

And the significance of what had occurred within it remained largely unseen.

Chapter 19

2022 — The First Disturbance

By the summer of 2022, Falcon Hollow had settled into a period of stability that residents rarely questioned. The years that followed the middle of the previous decade had passed without incidents that demanded sustained attention from the community. Daily life continued according to the patterns that had long defined the town's sense of order, and most residents experienced those years as uneventful in the most reassuring sense of the word.

The rhythms of the warmer months were particularly familiar. Visitors arrived to fish along the lake's quieter edges and to walk the wooded trails that wound through the hills west of town. Main Street businesses extended their hours to accommodate seasonal traffic, while the Gazette's summer editions reflected the small adjustments that accompanied the influx of visitors: increased park maintenance, occasional parking disputes, and the routine reminders that accompany a town temporarily sharing its quiet spaces with outsiders.

Within Falcon Hollow itself, the routines remained largely unchanged. The café on Cedar Street continued to serve as an informal gathering point for residents who preferred conversation before beginning their workdays. Local shops opened their doors to familiar customers whose habits had changed little over the years. Even the town's quieter spaces — the library, the walking paths near the lake, the benches around the town circle — followed the same patterns of use that had characterized them for decades.

In towns like Falcon Hollow, long stretches of calm can begin to feel permanent rather than temporary. Falcon Hollow was no exception. Residents spoke about the town's safety with a kind of quiet confidence, not because they believed disruption was impossible, but because experience suggested that serious disturbances tended to occur elsewhere.

It was against this backdrop that Falcon Hollow encountered an event during the early summer of that year that would gradually challenge those assumptions. The moment arrived without warning, as such moments often do, interrupting the town's routine in a way that residents initially struggled to interpret.

In the days that followed, conversations spread quickly through the informal networks that had long shaped how Falcon Hollow processed unusual news. People spoke about the incident in familiar settings — across café tables, along sidewalks outside Main Street shops, and in the small exchanges that occur when neighbors pause to compare what they have heard. Details circulated unevenly, sometimes contradicting one another, as they passed from one conversation to the next.

The uncertainty surrounding the event gave rise to speculation. Some residents attempted to interpret what had happened using explanations that felt consistent with the town's past experience. Others simply expressed disbelief that something so unsettling could have occurred within a place that had, for many years, appeared largely insulated from such disturbances.

The Gazette approached the situation with the caution typical of local reporting in small communities. Early coverage reflected the limited information available at the time, emphasizing confirmed details while avoiding conclusions that could not yet be supported. This approach was not unusual. Local newspapers often serve both as chroniclers of events and as participants in the social fabric they document, balancing the responsibility to report developments with an awareness of how those reports affect the community itself.

Official responses followed similarly measured patterns. Authorities addressed the matter through the procedures available to them, while town officials offered reassurances intended to preserve a sense of stability. In public statements, the emphasis remained on the belief that the incident represented an unusual but isolated occurrence.

For many residents, that interpretation proved reassuring. Communities often rely on the assumption that disruptive events are singular, particularly when no clear evidence suggests otherwise. Without an obvious connection to earlier incidents, the town had little reason to suspect that the moment belonged to anything larger.

Yet the disturbance lingered in Falcon Hollow's collective awareness longer than the event described in the town's earlier history. Conversations about the incident did not disappear as quickly as they had in previous years. Residents found themselves returning to the topic more frequently than usual, comparing notes and reconsidering details that might once have seemed insignificant.

Even so, the town did not yet recognize the event as part of a broader sequence. Without additional context, it remained difficult to interpret what had occurred beyond the boundaries of that single moment. Most residents continued to treat the incident as an anomaly — unsettling, certainly, but not necessarily indicative of a deeper problem within the community.

Over time, the rhythms of everyday life again began to assert themselves. Businesses reopened on their regular schedules, visitors continued to arrive for the summer season, and the Gazette gradually returned its attention to the municipal matters and seasonal activities that typically filled its pages. The disturbance did not vanish entirely from conversation, but it became less immediate as new concerns occupied the town's attention.

In retrospect, the year would later acquire a different meaning within Falcon Hollow's historical record. Residents who looked back on the period from the vantage point of subsequent events would recognize that the town had encountered something more significant than it understood at the time.

In 2022, however, that realization had not yet taken shape.

The community interpreted the moment in the most familiar way available to it — as a troubling but isolated interruption within an otherwise stable year.

The town had experienced a disturbance.

But it had not yet recognized that the disturbance might be part of something larger.

Chapter 20

2023 — The Uneasy Summer

By the summer of 2023, Falcon Hollow had largely resumed the rhythms that had defined the town for generations. The disturbance that had unsettled residents the previous year had not vanished entirely from conversation, but it had gradually settled into the category of events people referenced only occasionally — moments remembered with uncertainty but rarely examined in detail. Life in the town continued according to the patterns residents had long relied upon to organize their days.

Seasonal routines again shaped the community's calendar. Visitors arrived as the weather warmed, drawn by the same quiet landscapes that had long defined Falcon Hollow's reputation beyond its borders. The lake filled with anglers in the early mornings, hikers returned to the wooded trails that wound along the hills west of town, and Main Street businesses adjusted their schedules to accommodate the modest increase in summer activity.

The Gazette's pages reflected these familiar cycles. Coverage centered on the municipal matters that routinely occupied the town's attention: preparations for seasonal festivals, discussions at town council meetings, and the ordinary concerns of local governance. The newspaper's tone suggested a community continuing along its expected path, even as the memory of the previous year's disturbance lingered quietly beneath the surface of public awareness.

In many respects, the town's outward appearance remained unchanged. Residents gathered in the same places they always had. Conversations at the café on Cedar Street moved easily between local news, personal updates, and the small observations that accompany life in a place where people tend to know one another well. Shop owners greeted familiar customers, and the benches around the town circle again filled with people who had followed the same routines for years.

Yet beneath these familiar scenes, something subtle had begun to shift.

In Falcon Hollow, memory rarely disappears entirely. It simply waits for a moment when it becomes useful again. In Falcon Hollow, the earlier disturbance had not entirely faded from the town's consciousness. It existed as a reference point — not one that residents discussed constantly, but one that had quietly altered the way some people interpreted unusual developments.

When the town encountered another unsettling event during the summer of 2023, that earlier moment returned to conversation more quickly than it might have in previous years. Residents who heard the news often reacted with a familiar pattern of disbelief followed by speculation, but this time the speculation included comparisons that had not been widely voiced before.

People began recalling the previous year's disturbance in greater detail. Conversations that once treated that earlier moment as isolated now returned to it as a possible point of reference. The comparisons were rarely stated with certainty. More often they appeared in tentative language — suggestions offered cautiously, followed by acknowledgments that such connections might simply reflect coincidence.

This hesitation reflected a common instinct in communities unaccustomed to repeated disruptions. Residents may notice similarities between events, but they often resist drawing firm conclusions without clear evidence. The possibility that two unusual moments might share a deeper connection can feel unsettling in ways that speculation alone does not.

In Falcon Hollow, this instinct toward caution shaped the way the town discussed the situation throughout that summer. Conversations circulated through the same informal networks that had long carried news across the community, but they did so with a slightly different tone than before. People asked questions more frequently. They revisited details that might once have seemed insignificant. They compared what they had heard with what others believed to be true.

The Gazette reflected this shift with characteristic restraint. Reporting remained careful and measured, emphasizing confirmed developments while avoiding interpretations that extended beyond available information. Nevertheless, attentive readers could sense that the paper's coverage now carried a different weight. Stories that might once have been brief updates received greater attention, and references to the previous year's disturbance appeared more openly within the reporting.

Local officials responded in a similar manner. Public statements continued to emphasize stability and caution against premature conclusions, but the language surrounding those statements suggested a growing awareness that the town was confronting something more complex than it had first assumed.

For many residents, the summer of 2023 became a period defined less by certainty than by comparison. The town had not yet reached a point where it could confidently identify a pattern, but the possibility of such a pattern had entered public consciousness. Once introduced, that possibility proved difficult to ignore entirely.

The result was a subtle but noticeable shift in how Falcon Hollow interpreted unusual developments. Events that might once have been dismissed quickly were now examined more closely. Residents paid greater attention to the details that accompanied local news, even when those details seemed minor. Conversations lingered longer on subjects that might previously have passed with little comment.

At the same time, the town remained reluctant to abandon the assumptions that had shaped its understanding of safety for so long. Falcon Hollow had spent decades believing that serious disturbances belonged primarily to other places. The idea that such disruptions might appear repeatedly within the community challenged that belief in ways many residents were not yet prepared to accept.

As the summer progressed, everyday routines continued to anchor the town's sense of stability. Businesses operated on their normal schedules, seasonal visitors came and went, and the Gazette's pages eventually returned to covering the familiar topics that filled most editions. Outwardly, Falcon Hollow appeared much as it had in previous years.

Yet the conversations that unfolded quietly across the town suggested that something had begun to change.

The earlier disturbance no longer existed only as a memory. It had become a point of comparison — a moment residents now reconsidered when interpreting the events unfolding around them. The town had not yet concluded that the two incidents belonged to the same sequence, but the possibility had taken root in the community's awareness.

Looking back from the vantage point of later years, it becomes clear that the summer of 2023 marked the moment when Falcon Hollow first began to suspect that its earlier assumptions might require reconsideration.

The pattern itself had not yet been fully recognized.

But the town had started to look backward.

And once a community begins to reinterpret its past, the future rarely appears quite as predictable as it once did.

Chapter 21

2024 — When the Pattern Appeared

By the summer of 2024, Falcon Hollow had already spent two years quietly reconsidering its sense of stability. The disturbances that had unsettled the town in the previous summers had not disappeared from conversation in the way earlier incidents once had. Instead, they lingered in the background of civic awareness, returning periodically to discussion whenever residents found themselves searching for explanations that had yet to fully emerge.

The town's outward routines remained intact. Visitors still arrived during the warmer months to fish along the lake and to walk the wooded trails beyond the western ridge. Main Street businesses continued to operate according to the schedules that had sustained them for years, and the Gazette maintained its steady rhythm of reporting on municipal decisions, school activities, and the seasonal events that organized the town's calendar.

Yet the sense of continuity that had once accompanied these routines now carried a degree of tension that had not previously been present. Residents who gathered in familiar places found themselves returning more frequently to the disturbances that had unsettled the town during the previous two summers. Conversations that once treated those moments cautiously now examined them with greater confidence, as though the community had begun to accept that something about the pattern of events deserved closer attention.

This shift in perception did not occur suddenly. It developed gradually through the accumulation of conversations that unfolded across Falcon Hollow's informal networks. People compared what they remembered from earlier years with what they were hearing now. Details that had once seemed unrelated were reconsidered alongside one another. Observations shared quietly between neighbors found their way into wider discussions that extended beyond the places where they had first been voiced.

When another unsettling event occurred during the early summer of 2024, the town responded differently than it had in the years before.

Where earlier disturbances had produced uncertainty followed by cautious speculation, this moment produced a more immediate recognition that something larger might be unfolding. Residents who heard the news did not treat it simply as another isolated disruption. Instead, many of them instinctively looked backward — not only to the previous summer, but to the year before that as well.

For the first time, Falcon Hollow began to speak openly about the possibility that these moments were connected.

The language of conversation changed almost immediately. Where residents had once referred to earlier disturbances as singular incidents, they now began describing them together, placing them within the same line of discussion. The idea of coincidence — once the explanation most frequently offered — no longer satisfied the questions people found themselves asking.

This shift became visible in the town's public discourse as well. The Gazette's reporting, while still careful and measured, reflected the fact that the community was now considering events within a broader context. References to earlier years appeared more frequently within the paper's coverage, and readers could sense that the newspaper was documenting not only the moment itself but the growing realization that it belonged to a sequence.

Local officials responded with similar caution. Public statements continued to emphasize the need for patience and clarity, but the tone surrounding those statements suggested that the town had reached a point where previous assumptions could no longer remain entirely intact.

In small communities, recognition often arrives not through a single revelation but through the accumulation of shared observations. Individuals may notice connections independently, but it is only when those observations begin to circulate widely that the community as a whole acknowledges what they suggest.

Falcon Hollow reached that point during the summer of 2024.

Residents who had spent the previous year quietly comparing events now found themselves discussing those comparisons openly. The disturbances that had once appeared isolated were now described together, arranged in conversation as though they formed points along a line that had gradually come into view.

This realization did not immediately produce panic. The town's instinct for restraint remained strong, and many residents continued to approach the situation cautiously. Yet the atmosphere of uncertainty that had characterized earlier summers now gave way to something more definitive: the recognition that Falcon Hollow was confronting a pattern it had not previously understood.

The effects of this recognition appeared gradually across the routines of everyday life. People spoke about the disturbances more frequently, and they did so with a seriousness that had not accompanied earlier conversations. Visitors to the lake sometimes noticed that residents lingered longer than usual in discussions about recent developments. Shop owners on Main Street heard customers exchanging observations that would have seemed speculative only a year earlier.

Even the town's quieter spaces reflected the shift. Benches around the town circle hosted longer conversations than usual, and the café on Cedar Street found itself serving customers who arrived not only for their morning coffee but also to compare what they had heard from others.

None of these changes were dramatic on their own. Falcon Hollow remained outwardly calm, and daily routines continued to organize the community's life much as they always had. Yet beneath that surface, the town's understanding of itself had begun to evolve.

For many residents, the most unsettling aspect of the moment was not the individual disturbances themselves but the realization that those disturbances might belong together. Once the idea of a pattern entered public conversation, it proved difficult to ignore.

The town had spent decades believing that serious disruptions belonged primarily to other places. The events now being discussed suggested that Falcon Hollow might no longer be able to maintain that assumption without reconsideration.

Looking back, it becomes clear that the summer of 2024 marked the point at which the community's perception shifted most decisively. Earlier years had produced speculation and comparison, but this was the moment when Falcon Hollow began to recognize that those earlier observations had been pointing toward something larger.

The town had encountered disturbances before.

But now, for the first time, it understood them as part of the same story.

The years had become coordinates.

And Falcon Hollow had finally begun to see the line they formed.

Chapter 22

After the Silence

Communities rarely recognize the full meaning of events while those events are still unfolding. Understanding usually arrives later, once time has created enough distance for patterns to become visible. In Falcon Hollow, the years that residents would eventually come to view as connected did not appear that way when they were first experienced. Each moment entered the town's history separately, interpreted according to the habits and expectations that had long shaped how the community understood disruption.

Only afterward did those years begin to assemble themselves differently in the town's memory.

When Falcon Hollow looked back across that period, the earlier disturbances no longer appeared as isolated incidents scattered across otherwise ordinary summers. Instead, they began to resemble points within a sequence — moments that had quietly accumulated significance even while the town continued to interpret them individually.

This realization did not arrive all at once. It emerged gradually through the same informal networks that had first carried news of the disturbances through the community. Residents who had once spoken about the events cautiously now revisited them with a different sense of clarity. Conversations that had once relied on speculation began to draw more confidently upon shared recollection.

People remembered where they had first heard about each moment. They recalled the conversations that followed and the explanations they had once accepted as sufficient. What had previously seemed like unrelated occurrences now appeared within a different frame of reference, shaped by the knowledge that Falcon Hollow had experienced not one unusual year but several.

As these recollections circulated, the town began quietly reorganizing its understanding of that period.

This process affected more than individual memory. The community's public record began to reflect the same shift. The Gazette's coverage of the disturbances, once separated by months and years, was now read and discussed together. Articles that had originally appeared as routine reporting were reconsidered as part of a longer narrative that had only recently come into focus.

Such reinterpretation is not unusual in communities that experience unexpected disruptions. When events challenge established assumptions about safety and stability, residents often return to earlier moments searching for details they might have overlooked. The past becomes a resource through which the present can be understood.

Falcon Hollow followed this pattern. People revisited earlier conversations, sometimes discovering that fragments of the story had been present long before anyone recognized their significance. Observations that had once seemed minor or uncertain now appeared within a larger context that made them easier to interpret.

At the same time, the town remained reluctant to dramatize what had occurred. Falcon Hollow's culture had long favored restraint over spectacle, and that instinct continued to shape how residents discussed the disturbances even after their broader significance had been acknowledged. Conversations about the years in question were often reflective rather than sensational, emphasizing the ways the community had experienced the moments rather than the details that had originally made them unsettling.

This tone extended to the town's institutions as well. Public statements, newspaper coverage, and community discussions all reflected a similar preference for careful language. The emphasis remained on understanding what the sequence of events had meant for Falcon Hollow as a community rather than on revisiting the circumstances of each individual moment.

Over time, the disturbances gradually settled into the town's historical record.

This did not mean that Falcon Hollow forgot what had occurred. On the contrary, the years became reference points within the community's collective memory. Residents occasionally spoke about them when discussing how the town had changed or when explaining to newcomers why certain conversations carried a tone of quiet recognition that might otherwise seem difficult to interpret.

Yet the passage of time also allowed daily routines to reassert themselves. Businesses continued to open their doors each morning, visitors returned during the warmer months, and the Gazette resumed its familiar rhythm of reporting on the ordinary matters that typically occupy a small community's attention. The town's life moved forward, as it always had.

What changed was not the rhythm of Falcon Hollow but the way residents understood the continuity of that rhythm. The disturbances had introduced a new awareness that stability could not always be assumed simply because it had existed in the past.

Communities rarely abandon their habits entirely after such realizations. Instead, they incorporate new understanding into the frameworks that already organize daily life. Falcon Hollow did the same. The town retained its instinct for restraint and its reliance on the informal networks that had long shaped how information moved through the community. At the same time, residents carried a deeper awareness of how easily assumptions about safety could obscure patterns that only become visible with time.

This awareness influenced the way Falcon Hollow remembered the years that had unsettled it.

The events themselves remained part of the past — points that marked the gradual shift in how the community interpreted its own history. The events themselves remained part of the past, but the perspective they created continued to shape the town's conversations about the present.

Falcon Hollow had not become a different place.

Its streets, businesses, and public spaces remained the same. The café on Cedar Street still filled with early-morning conversations, the Gazette still arrived each week with reports on municipal matters, and the lake still drew visitors during the warmer months.

Yet the town now carried an additional layer of memory.

Residents who lived through those years understood that Falcon Hollow's history included moments when familiar assumptions proved incomplete. The disturbances had not erased the town's sense of stability, but they had complicated it in ways that would continue to influence how the community interpreted unusual events in the future.

In this sense, the years that Falcon Hollow once experienced separately had become something else entirely.

They had become part of the town's shared narrative — a sequence of moments through which the community gradually reconsidered its understanding of itself.

The silence that once surrounded those years had given way to reflection.

And in that reflection, Falcon Hollow had learned to recognize the line those years had quietly drawn across its history.

PART VI
WHAT REMAINS LEGIBLE

Recognition rarely concludes a community's story. Once events have been reconsidered and patterns acknowledged, daily life continues within the same streets, institutions, and routines that existed before. Falcon Hollow experienced this transition quietly. The disturbances that once unsettled the town did not transform its landscape or its habits, but they did introduce a deeper awareness into the rhythms that had long sustained it. The following chapters return to the town itself, observing how Falcon Hollow continues its ordinary life while carrying a clearer understanding of the years that reshaped its memory.

Chapter 23

After Recognition

Historical understanding rarely changes a community all at once. Recognition tends to arrive quietly, settling into conversation and routine rather than announcing itself through dramatic shifts in daily life. Falcon Hollow experienced this transition in much the same way it had processed earlier disturbances: gradually, through the accumulation of small adjustments that only became visible when viewed from a distance.

In the months following the summer in which the town began openly acknowledging the sequence of events that had unsettled it, Falcon Hollow appeared outwardly much as it always had. Visitors arriving along the two-lane road that curved into town encountered the same landscape that had greeted travelers for decades. Main Street businesses opened each morning, the Gazette continued its steady weekly publication, and the lake beyond the western edge of town reflected the same quiet mornings that had long drawn fishermen and walkers to its shoreline.

Yet the town's conversations carried a tone that had not existed in quite the same way before.

Residents who gathered in familiar places now spoke about unusual developments with a degree of attentiveness that suggested a subtle shift in how people interpreted what they saw around them. The disturbances that had once been discussed cautiously as isolated moments now existed within a shared understanding that Falcon Hollow's history contained periods of uncertainty as well as long stretches of calm.

This awareness did not dominate everyday conversation. Most discussions still revolved around the ordinary subjects that had always defined life in a town of Falcon Hollow's size: school events, local businesses, seasonal weather, and the countless small observations that accompany a community where neighbors recognize one another easily. But when unusual events did arise, residents approached them differently than they had in years past.

People listened more carefully.

They asked questions sooner.

And they were less inclined to dismiss unsettling developments as coincidences without first considering the possibility that patterns might exist beneath the surface of ordinary explanation.

These adjustments were subtle enough that many residents might not have noticed them if asked directly. Falcon Hollow had not adopted a new identity in response to the years that had unsettled it. The town's habits of restraint and its preference for quiet reflection remained firmly in place.

What had changed was not the town's character but the perspective through which that character now operated.

In conversations at the café on Cedar Street, residents occasionally referenced earlier summers in ways that suggested those moments had settled permanently into the town's shared vocabulary. People spoke about them without dramatization, often in the same tone used when recalling difficult winters or unexpected storms — events that had disrupted routine but had ultimately become part of Falcon Hollow's broader story.

The Gazette reflected this shift with characteristic subtlety. Coverage of local developments continued to emphasize the practical matters that typically occupied the newspaper's pages, yet attentive readers could sense that the paper now approached unusual events with a slightly different awareness. Reports carried an understanding that the town's recent history had complicated the assumption that every disturbance would prove temporary or isolated.

This change did not produce anxiety so much as attentiveness.

Falcon Hollow had learned that stability does not eliminate disruption. Instead, stability provides the framework within which disruption can be recognized and understood. The community's long-standing habits — careful conversation, measured reporting, and the informal networks through which residents shared information — remained the same. What had evolved was the way those habits interpreted the world around them.

For many residents, this shift appeared most clearly in the small moments that punctuated everyday life. A comment exchanged between neighbors might linger a little longer than it once had. An unusual observation might prompt a follow-up question that earlier years would have left unasked. Conversations that once moved quickly past unsettling topics now paused long enough to examine them more closely.

None of these moments altered the town's outward rhythm. Falcon Hollow continued to move through its days according to the patterns that had defined it for generations. Yet beneath that continuity lay a quiet recognition that the town's history had taught it something about how easily familiar assumptions could obscure the significance of unfolding events.

Communities rarely abandon their established ways of living after such realizations. More often, they incorporate new understanding into the habits that already organize daily life. Falcon Hollow did the same. The town retained its instinct for restraint, its reliance on local conversation, and its preference for interpreting events cautiously rather than dramatically.

What changed was the attention those habits now carried.

Residents who lived through the years that had unsettled Falcon Hollow understood that patterns sometimes appear only after time has allowed separate moments to align. That understanding did not transform the town into something new. Instead, it gave familiar routines a deeper sense of awareness.

Falcon Hollow continued much as it always had.

But it continued with a clearer understanding of the ways in which its own history had quietly unfolded.

154

But it continued with a clearer understanding of the ways in which its own history had quietly unfolded.

Chapter 24

The Durable Things

In Falcon Hollow, change is rarely measured by ordinary years but by the moments that interrupt them. Yet just as important as the disturbances that occasionally draw attention to a community are the elements that remain constant through those moments, continuing quietly while the town adjusts its understanding of what has occurred. In Falcon Hollow, these enduring elements shaped how the town absorbed the years that had unsettled it.

The physical landscape of the town offered the most immediate example of this continuity. The streets, buildings, and public spaces that had organized Falcon Hollow's daily life for generations remained largely unchanged. Main Street still formed the center of commercial activity, its storefronts opening each morning to the same sidewalks that had carried residents through countless ordinary days.

The café on Cedar Street continued to welcome early customers before the rest of the town had fully awakened. Conversations that began over coffee often drifted from local news to personal matters and back again, following the easy rhythm that had long defined those gatherings. The topics occasionally touched on the summers that had prompted the town's recent reflections, but more often they revolved around the practical concerns that occupy communities everywhere: work schedules, school activities, weather forecasts, and the quiet observations that accompany life in a place where neighbors recognize one another easily.

The Gazette maintained its familiar role within this landscape. Each week the paper arrived with its careful record of municipal life: council decisions, school events, business updates, and the countless small developments that collectively form the public memory of a town. Even during periods when Falcon Hollow found itself reconsidering the meaning of earlier disturbances, the Gazette continued documenting the ordinary matters that sustained civic life.

In towns like Falcon Hollow, the local newspaper performs a function that extends beyond simple reporting. It becomes a kind of civic ledger, recording not only the larger developments that occasionally interrupt routine but also the smaller decisions and conversations that gradually shape a community's character. Over time, these entries accumulate into a quiet archive of shared experience. Residents who read the paper each week may not think of it in these terms, yet the steady record it produces allows the town to remember itself with greater clarity than memory alone might permit.

Beyond the center of town, the natural features that had long defined Falcon Hollow's character remained unchanged as well. The lake continued to draw residents and visitors to its quiet shoreline, particularly during the early mornings when the water reflected the surrounding hills with almost complete stillness. Walkers followed the same wooded trails that had wound through the landscape for decades, and the fields beyond the town's outskirts shifted through the familiar cycle of seasons.

Places such as these often carry memory differently than the conversations that occur within them. A shoreline path or a familiar bench may witness countless exchanges without retaining the details of any single one. Yet the presence of these locations gives a community a sense of continuity that outlasts individual moments. Residents return to them year after year, sometimes aware that earlier discussions once unfolded in the same spaces, sometimes not. In this way the landscape itself becomes part of the town's quiet record.

These places gave Falcon Hollow a continuity that outlasted the years that unsettled it. Residents who moved through these spaces each day encountered reminders that the town's identity extended far beyond the disturbances that had recently drawn attention to its history. The café, the Gazette office, the quiet lakefront paths — each represented a form of stability that existed independently of the events that occasionally disrupted them.

Falcon Hollow's durability has never depended on dramatic gestures. It emerges instead from the steady repetition of routines that continue even when circumstances grow uncertain. Shop owners open their doors each morning because the town expects those doors to open. Newspapers print their pages each week because residents rely on that record to understand their shared life. Conversations take place in familiar locations because those places provide the setting through which community itself becomes visible.

What appears ordinary when experienced day by day often reveals its importance only in retrospect. The repeated actions that sustain a community — opening businesses, printing newspapers, attending council meetings, greeting familiar faces along the same sidewalks — form a structure that allows residents to interpret unusual events without losing their sense of continuity. Without these routines, disruption would feel far more destabilizing. With them, even unsettling moments can be placed within a broader framework of shared life.

Falcon Hollow possessed many such durable elements, and they quietly shaped how the town processed the years that had unsettled it. Residents who might otherwise have struggled to interpret the disturbances found reassurance in the continuity surrounding them. The physical and institutional structures of the town provided a framework within which uncertainty could be absorbed without overwhelming daily life.

Over time, these enduring features helped Falcon Hollow integrate the lessons of recent years into its broader sense of identity. The town did not forget what had occurred, but neither did it allow those events to define the entirety of its character. Instead, the disturbances became one thread within a much larger fabric — a fabric woven from routines, places, and relationships that had existed long before those years and would continue long afterward.

Walking through Falcon Hollow now, a visitor might notice little difference from the town that existed before those summers. The same storefronts line Main Street. The same quiet roads lead toward the lake. The Gazette still records the ordinary details of civic life with the same measured tone it has maintained for generations.

Yet the durability of these elements carries a deeper significance for those who know the town well. Residents understand that continuity does not mean the absence of disruption. Rather, continuity reflects the ability of a community to hold both stability and uncertainty within the same shared space.

In Falcon Hollow, the durable things — the places, institutions, and habits that structure daily life — remain the foundation upon which the town continues to move forward.

They do not erase what the town has experienced.

But they ensure that Falcon Hollow's story extends beyond any single chapter of its history.

Chapter 25

The Work That Doesn't Announce Itself

Communities are often remembered for the moments that interrupt their history. A dramatic event, a sudden disruption, or an unexpected sequence of years can appear to define how a town understands itself. Yet the greater portion of a community's life rarely unfolds in those moments. It exists instead in the quieter work that continues between them.

Falcon Hollow has always relied on this quieter work.

Much of it occurs without announcement. No formal recognition accompanies the routines that sustain the town from one day to the next. Residents simply perform them because the community expects them to be performed. Over time these repeated actions become so familiar that they are rarely noticed, even though they provide the structure within which every other part of the town's life takes place.

Each morning the same storefronts unlock their doors along Main Street. Deliveries arrive before most of the town has fully awakened, and lights appear behind shop windows that have opened in roughly the same order for years. Customers pass through these spaces not because anything unusual has occurred but because routine requires that daily life continue as it always has.

The Gazette operates according to a similar rhythm. Each week its pages are assembled with the same careful attention that has guided the paper through decades of municipal reporting. Articles record council discussions, school activities, and the practical matters that shape civic life. The work involved in producing these pages rarely attracts notice beyond the readers who expect the paper to arrive on schedule. Yet without that steady record, Falcon Hollow would have far fewer ways to understand the continuity of its own story.

Other forms of quiet work appear in places that rarely draw public attention at all. Someone clears fallen branches from a walking path before the morning's visitors arrive. A neighbor checks on an elderly resident whose porch light has not turned on at the usual time. A shop owner pauses during the afternoon to ask a passing customer about something mentioned in conversation the day before. None of these moments seem particularly significant on their own. Yet together they form the network of attentiveness that allows a community to recognize itself as a community.

Falcon Hollow has always depended on this network.

The years that unsettled the town did not alter the presence of these routines. If anything, they revealed how much of the town's stability rested upon them. Residents who had spent those years reconsidering the meaning of earlier disturbances gradually came to understand that the town's endurance was not the result of dramatic intervention or sudden transformation. It emerged instead from the quiet persistence of ordinary life.

People continued to gather at the café on Cedar Street, sometimes discussing the town's recent history but more often returning to the everyday topics that had always filled those tables. The lake still drew walkers during the early morning hours, and the Gazette continued to arrive each week with its careful documentation of municipal life. None of these routines required special attention to continue. They simply resumed the patterns that had sustained Falcon Hollow long before the years that had unsettled it.

This kind of continuity rarely announces itself. It does not appear in dramatic headlines or public ceremonies. Instead it reveals itself gradually through the accumulation of ordinary days in which the town continues to function according to its established rhythms.

Falcon Hollow's history contains moments that have drawn greater attention than others. The years that prompted the town's recent reflection will likely remain part of its shared memory for a long time.

Yet those years do not define the entirety of the community's story. They exist within a much longer sequence of days in which residents opened their businesses, printed their newspaper, walked their familiar paths, and greeted one another along the sidewalks of Main Street.

In the end, it is this quieter sequence that sustains a place like Falcon Hollow.

The work that maintains a town rarely calls attention to itself. It happens in small gestures repeated across days, weeks, and years, performed by people who may never think of those actions as particularly meaningful. Yet taken together, those gestures create the continuity that allows a community to endure through the moments that might otherwise seem to define it.

Falcon Hollow continues because its residents continue.

And in the steady repetition of their ordinary routines, the town's history moves forward — not through dramatic declarations, but through the quiet work of living.

EPILOGUE

Alignment

Nothing here concludes.

The town continues in the same manner it always has: through repetition so familiar that it rarely draws attention. Morning arrives along Main Street without announcement. Doors unlock in the same sequence they did yesterday. Coffee is poured before the first conversation reaches its full shape. The Gazette is assembled again, page by page, carrying forward the town's habit of recording what can be said clearly and leaving the rest to circulate elsewhere.

From the outside, Falcon Hollow appears unchanged.

Visitors still arrive along the two-lane road that descends gradually into the basin. The lake remains where it has always been, holding the western edge of town with the same quiet authority it exercised long before the first storefront faced the street. The gazebo still occupies the center of Town Circle. The café windows still gather early light before the sidewalks fill.

The town has not rearranged itself.

What has changed exists primarily in attention.

Residents who lived through the years that unsettled Falcon Hollow now move through these same spaces with a slightly different awareness of how the town's continuity operates. The habits that once felt automatic—containment, compression, patience—are recognized more easily as the structures they have always been.

People notice sooner when a conversation lingers longer than usual.

They notice when an observation travels quickly from one counter to another.

They notice when something unusual fails to settle as easily as earlier disruptions once did.

None of these adjustments alter the town's outward rhythm. Falcon Hollow remains what it has always been: a place organized less by declaration than by alignment. Streets still guide movement. Institutions still absorb pressure. Roles continue to exist regardless of who occupies them.

But the pattern is easier to see now.

The years that once appeared separately within the town's memory have taken on a different relationship to one another. Residents do not necessarily revisit those moments in detail. Falcon Hollow rarely operates that way. Instead, the years function as coordinates—quiet markers that now orient the town's understanding of how disruption can move through its landscape.

This awareness does not produce alarm.

It produces attention.

The café continues to host conversations that begin with weather and end somewhere less predictable. The lake continues to gather people along its shoreline at hours when the town is otherwise quiet. The Gazette continues documenting council decisions, school events, and the countless ordinary developments that compose civic life.

These routines persist because they remain useful.

Durability in Falcon Hollow has never required explanation. It depends instead on occupancy. Someone must continue unlocking the doors. Someone must continue printing the paper. Someone must continue noticing when a pattern begins to form.

The town does not require that these tasks be performed by the same people who carried them before.

Only that the positions remain filled.

Falcon Hollow has always produced placeholders more easily than legends. A counter must be kept. A record must be maintained. A place must remain open long enough for another person to rely on it tomorrow.

The individuals change.

The alignment remains.

This is why the disturbances that once unsettled the town have not redefined it. They did not replace Falcon Hollow's structures. They revealed them.

Containment remains possible.

Compression remains instinctive.

Routine still organizes the town's sense of time.

But these systems now exist beside a clearer understanding of their limits. Residents who once assumed that stability would persist indefinitely now recognize that continuity depends on attention as much as habit.

Falcon Hollow did not become a different place after those years.

It became a place that understands itself slightly better.

The basin still gathers weather. The streets still guide movement. The lake still reflects what stands beside it without commentary. These functions do not depend on interpretation.

They depend on persistence.

And persistence, in Falcon Hollow, has never required spectacle.

It requires only that someone remains long enough to hold a position steady while pressure passes through.

That work continues.

The town does not pause to announce it.

It simply resumes.

Nothing here concludes.

Falcon Hollow continues.